THIS WICKED GAME

MICHELLE ZINK

DIAL BOOKS
An imprint of Penguin Group (USA) LLC

DIAL BOOKS

Published by the Penguin Group

Penguin Group (USA) LLC

375 Hudson Street, New York, New York 10014

USA/Canada/UK/Ireland/Australia/New Zealand/India/South Africa/China

penguin.com

A Penguin Random House Company

Library of Congress Cataloging-in-Publication Data

Zink, Michelle.

This wicked game / by Michelle Zink.

p.   cm.

Summary: Seventeen-year-old Claire Kincaid, a descendant of Marie Leveau, is forced to embrace her voodoo heritage when mysterious strangers threaten to use an age-old curse to destroy her family and the boy she loves.

ISBN 978-0-8037-3774-7 (hardcover)

[1. Voodooism—Fiction. 2. Blessing and cursing—Fiction. 3. Faith—Fiction.
4. Revenge—Fiction. 5. New Orleans (La.)—Fiction.] I.Title.

PZ7.Z652Wic 2013   [Fic]—dc23   2012039102

Printed in the United States of America

1 3 5 7 9 10 8 6 4 2

Designed by Nancy R. Leo-Kelly

Text set in Dante

For Nancy Conescu,
who has made me better in so many ways

THIS
WICKED
GAME

ONE

Claire was at the front of the store, uploading a new batch of photographs while a pot of wax melted behind her, when the woman entered through the unmarked door.

It wasn't unusual for customers to use the private entrance. Other than the staircase leading to the house, the door was the only way in, and there were plenty of people in New Orleans who had a key.

But Claire had never seen the woman before, and that was unusual, especially since she had been working in the store since before she was tall enough to see over the counter.

Claire turned down the temperature on the wax and closed her laptop as the woman approached the counter. She was startlingly beautiful, her milky skin contrasting with the red lipstick that shaped her full mouth. Her clothes were expertly tailored, the white button-down nipped in at the waist, the hem of her navy trousers just grazing the floor as she walked.

Claire wiped her hands on a towel. "Hello. May I help you?"

"Good afternoon." The woman's voice was low and gravelly. Claire figured her for a heavy smoker. Either that or a 1940s film star. "I have some things I'd like to purchase."

"Sure." Claire pulled out the yellow notepad they used for orders.

The woman opened her slim black handbag and pulled out a folded piece of paper. She pushed it across the counter with one neatly manicured hand.

Claire opened it, glancing at the long list of items. It was a big order, and Claire immediately started transferring the woman's list to the notepad.

"This is your family's establishment?" The woman asked the question with the certainty of someone who already knew the answer.

"Uh-huh." Claire had to resist the urge to add "unfortunately" at the end of the sentence.

Frankincense, black cat oil, aniseed, aloeswood powder . . .

"It's quite a store. It seems you have everything."

"Just about," Claire said. A strand of her long blond hair fell forward. She tucked it behind one ear and continued transcribing the woman's list.

"And how long does it usually take to fill an order?" the woman asked.

"It depends on what you need. Let's see . . ." Claire scanned the list. Everything on the front page was in stock. She turned the paper over to the back. "We should be able to do this while you . . ."

The words stopped as she came to the last item on the list.

Two (2) vials black Panthera pardus *plasma.*

She felt her face flush as she searched her memory.

"Is there a problem?" the woman asked.

Claire didn't know if it was paranoia or something else, but she thought there was something new in the woman's voice. As if she'd known all along that the Kincaids wouldn't have the plasma and had enjoyed putting Claire through her paces.

Claire shook her head, resisting the urge to call out for her mother. Pilar Kincaid had little patience for Claire's "lack of commitment" to the family business. Calling her would only highlight Claire's inability to handle the store on her own. Besides, her knowledge of the craft wasn't exactly encyclopedic. Maybe she was wrong, but as far as she knew, black panther blood was only used for one thing.

Killing people.

"Um . . . not a problem. But one of these items might take us a while to get in. I think it's a special order."

"And which item would that be?"

"The black panther plasma. We don't keep it in stock."

No one keeps it, Claire thought. As far as the Guild was concerned, there were some things you just didn't mess around with, even if you were an experienced practitioner.

The woman tapped her manicured nails on the wood counter. "How long do you expect it will take to get it?"

"I'm not sure . . . Maybe a week?"

The woman didn't hesitate. "Fine. I'll take the rest of the items now."

Claire nodded. Everything else on the list was in stock, and she busied herself filling vials with the powder and herbs and wrapping roots in brown paper. She could feel the woman's eyes on her while she worked. It made the tiny hairs at the back of her neck stand on end and caused a prickling sensation behind her eyes.

Once the order was filled, she turned around, half expecting the woman to have transformed into some kind of monster.

But she was just the same, her gaze unflinching, her eyes so dark they were almost black.

"Here you go." Claire pushed the package toward the woman and turned to the calculator, wishing for the millionth time that they could join the twenty-first century and get a computer system for the store. She consulted the notepad, her fingers flying over the keys. "That'll be $357.42, without the panther plasma."

She had a hard time even saying it. Questions were drumming through her mind. She needed to get upstairs to her mother. She would know what to do.

The woman nodded slowly, pulling a wallet from her handbag and removing four hundred-dollar bills.

Claire took the money and made change from the lockbox they kept under the counter. "Would you like us to call you when we find out about the special order item?"

"That won't be necessary. I'll see you one week from today." She took her change and picked up the package. "Good-bye, Claire."

The woman turned and left through the private entrance. Claire watched the door shut behind her, listening for the click of the automatic lock. For a minute, she was rooted to the floor, wondering if she'd imagined the whole thing. Then she looked down at the list of items.

Two (2) vials black Panthera pardus *plasma.*

She took the stairs two at a time.

ﺍﻟﻠﻪ

The Kincaids' living quarters were separated from the store by one floor and a two-level staircase. Just a few months ago, the door between the two spaces hadn't even had a lock, but after a rash of break-ins, the Guild families who had stores on-site had taken measures to protect their private quarters from the customers who had access to the supply houses.

The world was changing, Claire's mother had said as the locksmith installed a heavy dead bolt on the door that separated the store from the two floors above it. Once a secret, old-school voodoo society, the Guild of High Priests and Priestesses had become too large for them to know each and every member. Now, it was up to the regional leaders to vet and approve applicants based on lineage and practice.

Claire reached the top of the stairs and fumbled through her keys for the one that fit the new lock. When she found it, silver and strangely shiny compared to the old ones that were for the house and store, she unlocked the door and hurried into the main hall of the house. "Mom? Where are you?"

She checked the drawing room first. The floor to ceiling windows were open to the terrace, the sheer draperies moving slightly in the barely there July breeze. The room was empty.

There was only one other place her mother would be if she wasn't in the drawing room, going over the accounts for the store or writing notes to Guild members who lived outside the city, and that was upstairs.

When Claire reached the second-floor landing, she continued down the hall, past her bedroom, her parents' room, two guest rooms, and an extra bathroom.

She stopped at a closed door at the end of the hall, listening to the gentle murmur of her mother's voice. The smell of burning incense drifted through the crack under the door.

Claire hesitated. She'd been about four years old when she'd first come upon her mother in this room. She had been wearing a white floor-length garment that Claire would later learn was standard ritual garb. The simple cotton tunic made her mother look taller and younger than she did in her everyday clothes. Her dark hair was long and loose around her shoulders as she kneeled in front of the altar, covered with burning white candles, wax figures, and dried herbs.

Claire had been afraid. The strange words that came from her mother's mouth frightened her, however softly they were spoken, and the flickering candles cast unfamiliar shadows.

Claire had avoided the room ever since.

But she couldn't avoid it now, and she rapped softly on the door, turning the knob and pushing the door open.

Her mother was there, in the same position Claire had found her all those years ago, kneeling in front of the tea table that served as an altar. This time she was in her regular clothes. The altar was alight with purple candles that meant her mother was either working a spirituality rite or trying to channel her power more effectively. Two sticks of incense burned on either side of a Bible, their smoke rising into the air in abstract swirls.

Her mother didn't look up or acknowledge her daughter's presence in any way. Claire waited a few seconds before she finally gave up and started talking.

"Mom, I—"

"You know I won't speak to you until you come in properly, Claire." Her mother didn't look away from the altar. Her hair, still long and black as a raven's wing, tumbled down over one of her shoulders. "Besides, aren't you supposed to be working the counter?"

Claire stepped into the room, but just barely. "I was, but—"

Now her mother looked over at her. "Then what are you doing up here? You know you're not supposed to leave the store unattended."

Claire crossed the room, her throat closing against the heavy scent of amber. She held out the piece of paper with the list of ingredients the woman had ordered.

Her mother took it, her gray eyes scanning the first page.

"These are all basic ingredients, Claire." She turned it over. "Surely you know how to . . ." Her voice trailed off. She shook her head, her face two shades paler than it had been when Claire had entered the room. "Where did you get this?"

"That's what I've been trying to tell you," Claire said. "A woman just came in. She gave me this order to fill."

Her mother rose to her feet, pacing to the fireplace. "Which client was it?"

"That's the thing," Claire said. "I've never seen her before."

Her mother turned to face her. "Then how did she get in?"

"With a key," Claire said simply.

"Are you sure the door was latched? That it was locked when she came in?"

Claire sighed. She didn't blame her mother for doubting her. She wasn't exactly attentive on the job. But still.

"Yes, Miss Julie was the last person to place an order, and the door locked behind her, just like always."

"Did this woman give you a name?"

No, Claire almost said, *but she knew mine.*

She didn't say it though. The woman had probably been told about the Kincaids by whoever referred her to the store.

Claire shook her head. "And I didn't ask. You've always told me not to. That if they have a key, I fill the orders, and that's it."

Her mother consulted the list again before looking up to meet Claire's eyes. "But this is . . . this is impossible."

She was still standing there, a look of shock on her face, when the phone rang.

"I'll get it." Claire left the room and picked up the phone that sat on a table in the hall. "Kincaid residence, Claire speaking."

"Hello, Claire." She immediately recognized the voice on the other end of the line. "May I speak to your mother or father, please? It's urgent."

"One moment." Claire covered the mouthpiece and went back to the ritual room, holding out the phone to her mother. "It's Aunt Estelle," she said quietly. "She says it's urgent."

Estelle Toussaint wasn't a blood relative to the Kincaids, but all the women in the Guild were Claire's "aunts," just as her mother was "Aunt Pilar" to the other Guild members' children.

Pilar smoothed her skirt, as though the caller could see her through the phone. "Hello, Estelle." Her mother paused, turning her back on Claire. "Well, I . . . When?" Another long pause. "Today?"

She didn't say anything else for a couple of minutes. Claire was beginning to wonder if her mother was still on the phone when she murmured a few quiet words into the mouthpiece. Then she turned around, avoiding Claire's eyes as she finished the call.

"Yes, I understand. We'll see you then." She hung up

the phone, staring at it like it was something she'd never seen before.

"Mom?" Claire said. "What's going on?"

Her mother looked up like she'd just realized Claire was still there. "We weren't the only ones who received a troubling order today."

"What do you mean?" Claire asked.

But her mother was already rushing from the room. "An emergency meeting has been called. Be ready to leave at six."

TWO

Unlike the other kids in the Guild, Claire had never wanted to be invited to a meeting of its leadership. It was tradition for the firstborns to be brought into the fold sometime after their eighteenth birthday, but since Claire wasn't eighteen until April, she'd hoped to put them off long enough to escape to college.

But now there was no avoiding it. An alarm had been sounded that echoed through the Guild, and a few hours later, Claire was in the backseat of their Lexus as her dad drove toward the Toussaint house, her mother silent and tense in the front seat beside him.

Claire was looking out the window, wishing she hadn't been the one working when the woman placed her order, when her phone vibrated in her pocket.

She pulled it out, fully expecting to see a text from her best friend, Sasha.

WHAT'S GOING ON?

Sasha always wanted to know what was going on inside the Guild, probably because her parents never told her anything. Christopher and Pauline Drummond wanted their daughter to focus on the craft, not the politics of the organization that supplied it. That would come with time, they told her. When she fully understood the importance of her heritage.

NOT GOING TO BELIEVE THIS, Claire typed. ON WAY TO GUILD MEETING.

Sasha's response came less than a minute later: ????!!!!

SOMEONE PLACED AN ORDER FOR AN ITEM ON THE BLACKLIST. I WAS WORKING THE COUNTER WHEN IT CAME IN.

WHAT WAS IT?????

Claire hesitated, wondering if she could get in trouble for telling Sasha. She started typing a second later.

BLACK PANTHER PLASMA. WILL GIVE YOU DETAILS LATER.

Claire put away her phone and looked out the window as they entered the Garden District. Her eyes swept upward to the great oaks that rose above them on either side, practically meeting in the center of the street.

She loved the Garden District. With its majestic old

houses, massive trees, and old-fashioned streetcars, it was a throwback to a gentler time. That the Toussaints, the most powerful family in an underground organization devoted to the craft of voodoo, lived in one of the mansions on First Street was an irony few would appreciate.

"I hope Estelle doesn't blame us for this," Claire's mother was saying from the front seat.

"Why on earth would she blame us?" Claire could almost see her dad rolling his eyes. "We weren't the only ones who got an order."

"Yes, but we were one of only three," Claire's mother said. "And you can bet they'll find a way to make it our fault."

It was an old argument. Claire's dad, Noel, was an optimist when it came to human nature, choosing to believe that every slight was a misunderstanding and every catastrophe the result of a simple mistake.

Pilar, on the other hand, was not so forgiving.

Then again, it was easier for her dad not to care what the Guild members thought about them. As a great-grandson of Marie Leveau, the most famous voodoo queen in history, his membership was a birthright. But for her mother, a poor bayou priestess with no heritage to speak of, it mattered. She could never seem to shake the suspicion that their role as outcasts was the result of Noel's marrying her.

Claire thought the prejudice was more about her. Despite the powerful blood running through her veins, she had shown as little aptitude for and interest in the craft as her father. To the members of the Guild, she was proof that the Leveau reign was dead.

Her father pulled through the scrolled iron gates leading to the Toussaint estate. The house came into view at the end of the drive, eight cars parked near the old carriage house at the back of the property. Her dad parked behind a familiar black Mercedes, and they climbed out of the car and headed toward the front door.

The Toussaint yard was perfectly maintained, the jasmine along the walkway and wild honeysuckle near the front portico scenting the air with heavy perfume. The house was one of the oldest in the District, its large columns perfectly spaced along the terrace and rising all the way up to the elaborate cornices at the roofline.

"Mrs. and Mrs. Kincaid." Betsy, the Toussaint's housekeeper, opened the door, waving them in. "The rest are in the library. I'll see you in."

Betsy led them down the hall, the wood floors polished to a high shine. They were almost to the library when little Sophie rounded the corner at a dead run, black hair bouncing on her tiny shoulders. She skidded to a stop when she spotted them.

"Claire!" Ignoring Betsy's good-natured but obvious disapproval, Sophie grabbed Claire's legs in a hug.

"Hey, pip-squeak," Claire said, bending over to squeeze the Toussaints' six-year-old daughter.

She and Sophie had a mutual admiration society. Sophie was always underfoot, always in trouble with Betsy, and always uninterested in the Guild's business. Claire couldn't help wondering if Sophie would grow up to be as apathetic as she was about voodoo.

Sophie gazed up at Claire. "You're coming to the ball, right? I have a new dress!"

Claire nodded reluctantly. The Guild's annual Priestesses' Ball was in two days, and while it was far from her favorite event, there was no way she could skip it.

"Claire has a new dress, too," Pilar interjected, smiling indulgently at Sophie.

"Okay, now," Betsy said, swatting at the little girl with a dish towel. "Get! And if you don't stay out from under my feet, I'm going to put you to work."

Sophie stepped away from Claire. "Bye, Claire. See

you at the ball!" She skipped toward the kitchen at the back of the house.

They continued down the hall to a pair of carved double doors. Betsy pushed them open and stepped into the library.

"Mrs. Toussaint, the Kincaids have arrived."

Estelle Toussaint, her chestnut hair perfectly coiffed into a tight bun, rose from a chair by the mantel. "Thank you, Betsy."

Claire felt an irrational burst of panic as Betsy left the room, as if the rotund woman could somehow protect her from the vipers in the Guild.

"Come in, come in," Estelle waved them in, advancing on them with a drink in one hand. "We've all had *quite* a day."

Claire's mother murmured sympathetically while her dad joined the others near the fireplace. Estelle came toward Claire, taking her chin in one hand. Claire wanted to swat it away, but she was paralyzed by the look in the woman's eyes and the utter silence that had descended on the rest of the room.

"My goodness!" Estelle said. "You've had a lot of excitement today, haven't you?" She surveyed Claire, as if daring her to disagree.

"Yes, ma'am."

"Well, Claire." She dropped her hand. "It seems you've secured your first Guild meeting early. Come have a seat with the others, dear."

Claire looked around the room. There were Julia and Reynaud St. Martin. They owned a wholesale store in the business district and were one of three families that occupied seats of power in the Guild, together with the Toussaints, who ran everything, and Claire's parents, who were just figureheads because of her father's lineage. The St. Martins' daughter, Allegra, was a gorgeous brunette rumored to have a powerful gift for the craft.

Claire let her eyes roam.

Delphine and Armand Rousseau, who ran the regional store for the nearby suburb of Metairie and didn't have any children, sat on the sofa at the center of the room. Next to them were Inez and Gabriel Morgan. They owned most of the stores at the outer reaches of the city. Claire had always liked their oldest daughter, Laura, a quiet redhead with a shy smile.

There was Charles Valcour—a widower for as long as Claire could remember—and the Valcour twins, Charles Junior and William, who had just returned from college. Bridget Fortier was at the sideboard pouring herself a drink, probably still recovering from a messy divorce that had almost cost the Guild their much-coveted discretion. Bridget had inherited her father's supply house after his death in a plane accident when she was just twenty-two years old. Despite her legendary temper, Claire couldn't help feeling sorry for the woman. Raising eight-year-old Daniel alone couldn't be easy. He was a "pistol," as Claire's dad liked to say.

The group was rounded out by Sasha's parents, Christopher and Pauline Drummond, standing near the wall by the fireplace. They ran a members-only store not unlike the Kincaids. Claire smiled as they raised a hand in greeting.

She didn't know how many members the Guild actually had—probably hundreds if not thousands. But these eight families were the ones who managed, ran, and controlled the supply houses and made policy to guide the organization's rules and practices.

Claire had known them her whole life.

Her eyes came to rest on Alexandre Toussaint, Sophie's big brother, leaning against the wall by the piano. On him, the posture looked sexy instead of lazy. He gazed at her from under thick lashes, and Claire had the feeling that he knew exactly what she'd been thinking while his mother had scrutinized her. Like Claire, he was seventeen, but he'd bypassed the formal-invite-on-your-eighteenth-birthday rule by virtue of his last name and address. All the Guild meetings were held at the Toussaint house, and Claire had never heard anyone question Xander's presence.

Pilar moved over on one of the love seats and motioned to her daughter. "Sit, Claire."

Having no choice but to play the dutiful daughter, Claire did. Besides, she had to admit to a grudging sense of comfort from being near her mother.

"Now, is everybody settled?" Estelle asked, looking around. She continued without waiting for an answer. "Good. Let's get started then." She turned to her husband. "Bernard."

Bernard Toussaint rose, standing in front of the fireplace. Looking at him, it was easy to see where Alexandre had gotten his good looks. Bernard's father had come to Louisiana from Haiti and married a rebellious Spanish heiress, a gene pool that had endowed his progeny with imposing stature, skin the color of caramel, and slightly exotic features.

But despite Bernard's commanding presence, everyone knew it was Estelle who ran things behind the scenes.

It wasn't that unusual. The room was full of powerful women accustomed to sheathing their strength in velvet gloves. In the South—and in the world of voodoo—it was the women who really ruled.

"Good evening," Bernard started. "Thank you all for coming on such short notice. I know our next meeting isn't scheduled for two more weeks, but a situation has arisen that requires our immediate attention."

Everyone shifted in their seats, a few casting glances at Claire. Given her attendance, it was only natural to think she had something to do with the impromptu gathering.

"This afternoon, three of the Guild's supply houses received orders for a blacklisted item. The orders came in at precisely the same time—one through the St. Martins' warehouse, one through one of our stores, and one through the Kincaids' house. In each case, the customers in question had a key that garnered them access through the private entrances, though a preliminary investigation reveals that none of the clients in question have frequented the Guild stores in the city before today."

"What was it?" Bridget asked from a chair by the fireplace. "The blacklisted item."

Bernard hesitated, and Claire wondered if he would

actually say it out loud. Even she knew it would cause panic.

Bernard continued. "The clients in question each placed large orders which included, among other things, the blood of black *Panthera pardus*."

A gasp escaped from the room, followed by an escalating murmur.

Bernard held up one hand. "Please. I know you're all alarmed, but we're here to compare notes so that we can better understand the nature of the orders."

"Better *understand* it? What's to understand?" Julia St. Martin asked. "Black panther's blood hasn't been routinely used for at least a century." She lowered her voice. "And with good reason."

Bernard nodded. "Absolutely. But since I have your account of the event at the St. Martin facility, and I have the one phoned in to Estelle and me from the store on Lafayette, let's hear Claire's version, as well, shall we?"

It was a rhetorical question, and Julia sat up straighter, smoothing her skirt like that would eliminate the wrinkles from her pride.

"Claire." Bernard waved her forward. "Please."

Claire rose reluctantly. Making her way to the fireplace, she was torn between regret that she hadn't listened to her mother and put on something more "appropriate" than shorts and a tank top and a vague sense of triumph that she'd stood her ground. At least she'd had the sense to twist her hair into a long braid.

She stood next to Bernard.

"Please explain what happened when the woman came in," Bernard coached.

Claire took a deep breath and recounted the chain of events, starting with the woman's entrance through the private door and continuing with her order and Claire's explanation that there would be a delay for the panther's blood.

When she was done, she hesitated, thinking about the woman's use of her name, wondering if it was important enough to mention.

"Is there anything else?" Estelle prompted. "Anything at all?"

Sighing, she decided she might as well tell them everything so they could take it from here.

"The woman knew my name."

Her father stood up, shock registering on his face as everyone else talked over each other.

Bernard held up a hand to quiet them. "What do you mean, Claire?"

She shrugged. "Right before she left, she called me by my first name."

"And you're sure you've never seen her before?" Gabriel Morgan asked.

Claire nodded, thinking about the woman's distinctive clothing, her cold, dark eyes. "I think I would have remembered her."

"Is there anything else you can tell us about the woman?" Julia demanded. "The other clients who placed orders were men."

Claire thought about it. "Not really. I mean, she was pretty and . . . I don't know, kind of glamorous, I guess."

"Pretty and glamorous?" Julia said, disbelieving. "How are we supposed to identify her with *that?*"

"I don't know. I'm sorry." Claire paused. "She did say that she would come back next week, though."

"Next week!" Julia exclaimed.

Claire's mother turned to Julia. "Claire did the best she could under the circumstances."

Noel placed a hand on his wife's knee. Claire recognized the gesture as one designed to rein in her mother's notorious temper.

Good luck with that, Dad.

"I know we're all . . . disturbed by this news," Bernard

said, "but Claire did the only thing she could without raising an alarm. She filled the order without question and went right to Pilar. It's all any of us could hope for in such a situation."

"Wouldn't it have been better to raise an alarm while she was still there?" Charlie Valcour asked, his pale face and blue eyes calling to mind nothing of the stereotypical voodoo families of old. "I mean, then she would have left, right?"

Charlie's father, Charles Senior, heaved a resigned sigh. "Then the woman wouldn't have come back. And if she doesn't come back, we won't have another chance to identify her or find out why she wants the panther blood."

Charlie flushed, his skin turning pink under his freckles.

"I think we all know why she wants it," Claire's mother said. "There's only one reason anyone would."

"But it's forbidden." Delphine Rousseau's voice was almost a whisper, and the room instantly quieted. Claire guessed that's what happened when you didn't talk much. People listened when you did.

"And if the woman entered through the locked door," Delphine continued, "she must be a member of the

Guild on some continent. Why would she risk expulsion?"

"Well now, that's something we don't know yet, isn't it?" Julia's voice was snide, and Delphine seemed to shrink a little inside her tailored suit.

The room erupted into noise as everyone volunteered theories about the motive behind the orders.

Claire, grateful for the opportunity to escape, took advantage of the chaos by edging to the door. Her mother was the only one who noticed, though she didn't say anything as Claire slipped into the hallway.

Making her way to the back of the house, Claire continued through the kitchen, where Betsy was banging around in one of the cupboards. Claire opened the back door as quietly as she could and stepped off the terrace, heading toward the arbor at the rear of the property.

It was quiet, the air almost liquid with summer heat and humidity. She followed the winding path, not wanting to risk Estelle's wrath should she accidentally step on the flowers, and took a seat at the big iron table.

"Bad luck, huh?"

The voice came from behind her. Claire turned to see Alexandre Toussaint standing at the entrance to the arbor.

She rolled her eyes. "That's an understatement."

He came toward her, the setting sun turning his skin golden. He held out a hand, pulling her to her feet when she took it. His arms snaked around her waist.

"I wondered why you didn't text me back," he said, looking down at her.

"Sorry. I was a little preoccupied."

"No kidding." His eyes, as smooth and liquid as chocolate, appraised her. "You okay?"

"Why wouldn't I be?'

He shrugged, his lithe but muscular shoulders pulling on the buttons of his shirt. "I was worried when I heard."

"About the customer?" Claire forced a laugh, pushing away the memory of the woman using her name. "She was probably just thinking she could kill her ex or something."

"She knew your name," he said.

"She could have gotten that anywhere," Claire said. "You know, with Marie and all."

It was true. Claire didn't like to think about strangers knowing who she was just because of her great-great-grandmother, but anyone with some persistence and an internet connection could probably trace Marie's genealogy to the Kincaids.

He brushed a loose strand of hair back from her face. "I worry about you."

She smiled. "Don't. I'm fine."

"So you always say." He leaned in until his lips were just inches from hers. "How long do you think they'll be busy?" he asked, referring to their parents and the rest of the Guild leadership.

"Long enough."

He kissed her, his mouth conforming perfectly to hers. She never stopped being surprised at the feeling that arose between them. They'd known each other their whole lives and had been dating in secret for over a year, but somehow the rush of desire she felt in his arms hadn't dimmed even a little.

He reluctantly pulled away, looking into her eyes. "Claire . . ."

She was bracing herself for the question she knew would follow when the sound of shoes crunching on gravel alerted them to someone's approach. They pulled apart just as Xander's mother arrived.

"There you are!" Estelle said, her gaze skimming over them. "We've been looking all over for you two."

"I'm sorry," Claire said. "It's my fault. I just . . . I needed some air. Xander was nice enough to check on me."

"I'm sure you've had quite a fright." Despite her words, Estelle didn't look sympathetic. Her gaze slid to her son. "Thank you for checking on Claire, Alexandre. Let's escort her back to the house, shall we? Her parents are ready to leave."

Estelle turned around, heading up the pathway. Claire and Xander followed behind her, careful to keep their distance in her company.

THREE

Claire knew things were bad by how little her parents said on the way home. She tried to get something out of them by asking what the Guild planned to do, but her mother just said that everything was under control and not to worry.

Which was fine with her. Claire had done her part. Maybe they would leave her out of it now.

It was after nine when they got home. Her parents headed straight for the study, where they would no doubt hash out every detail of what had happened at the Toussaints'. Claire was halfway up the stairs to her room when she realized she'd never closed up the shop for the day.

She stood there, her conscience warring with her mental exhaustion, before finally turning around.

As much as she didn't want to count the money and clean up the store, she didn't want her parents to have to do it either. Their night was probably even worse than hers.

Besides, Claire hadn't bolted the door before they'd left for the Toussaints,' and she doubted anyone else had either. The woman who'd ordered the panther's blood was proof that not everyone who had a key was a friend, and the Kincaids didn't have a security system like the one at the Toussaints'.

Downstairs, everything was like she left it. The lamps were even still on. She went to the door, pulling the big wooden bar across it. It was the only time they were really off-limits to the voodoo community.

She went to the counter, pulled out the lockbox, and started counting the money. Despite her lack of interest in the craft, she was happy that business was good. Suddenly, it seemed everyone was interested in alternatives to traditional medicine, traditional religion, traditional everything.

And those alternatives included voodoo.

From lighting purple candles for insight to burning herbs for health to wearing gris-gris bags as a talisman against evil, people wanted to believe there was something else in the world, something that couldn't be explained by science or conventional religion.

Finished counting, Claire turned off the wax, cursing when she realized she would have to start over making the small forms. Sometimes people bought the wax raw and shaped the ritual figures themselves, but the Kincaids also sold them ready-made. Claire hated the way it smelled and the residue it left on her skin, but it was a staple of their business.

She surveyed the store, her eyes traveling over the ochre-colored walls. Everything was more or less the way her mother liked it. Jars and bottles containing various powders, elixirs, oils, and seeds were neatly labeled on grid-like shelves, while the more exotic ingredients, including adder's-tongue, black hen's egg, and devil pod, were locked up in a case that ran the length of the counter. Gris-gris bags and bolts of red flannel were stacked at the front of the store, ritual garments neatly folded on the shelves. Bins and barrels held incense, sandalwood, lengths of devil's string, coffin nails, and the ready-made forms that were called doll babies by real voodoo practitioners—a deceptively innocent name for something said to cause so much damage—and voodoo dolls by everyone else, stared back at her, their expressionless faces eerie in the low light.

The weirdest thing about it was how unweird it was to Claire.

Sighing, she grabbed a broom and started to sweep the tile floors. It was the only job in the store she didn't mind. It was soothing, moving the broom back and forth, the scent of incense hanging like a ghost in the room. Her mind wandered, landing not on the woman who had ordered the panther blood but on Xander.

She almost couldn't remember what it was like when they were just friends, back when they only saw each other at Guild functions or at school. The change had been so subtle she hadn't noticed it at first. He'd stop by when his parents had messages for Claire's or drop off special orders from the Toussaint stores instead of having a delivery service do it. It had taken her a while to catch on.

Until one day, she did.

He'd caught up to her as she was leaving the store. She'd known it was intentional even though he said he was just passing by, and they'd gone to Marco's for pizza and talked for three hours. After that, being together had felt inevitable. It wasn't right or wrong.

It just was.

She pushed the broom under the counter, where powder, herbs, and wax shavings sometimes dropped. She was brushing everything into a pile when a piece of paper caught on the leg of the counter. She tried to use the broom to free it, but it was stuck. She finally bent down and pulled the scrap free.

It was a receipt. At the top was a picture of a computer and the words NEW ORLEANS NETWORKING SERVICES. Underneath it was a name and address:

Eugenia Comaneci

548 Dauphine Street

Claire stared at the name. There were very few clients she didn't know, and she didn't know Eugenia Comaneci. Which meant the receipt could only belong to the woman who'd ordered the panther blood.

Claire looked at the slip of paper a few seconds longer before stuffing it into the pocket of her shorts. She would show it to her mom tomorrow. Or maybe to her dad, who probably wouldn't freak out as much.

She swept the rest of the debris into the dustpan and threw it in the trash. Then she turned off the lamps and headed upstairs.

It was already hot and humid when she left the house the next morning, and she was glad she'd put her hair into a messy bun. She was meeting Sasha for yoga at 2:00 p.m., but had a stop to make first that would take her to another part of the city. Even biking, she'd be drenched by the time she got there.

She slung her messenger bag over her head, letting it fall across her body. It smacked against her leg as she left through the kitchen door and made her way along the side of the house.

Using her Guild key, she unlocked the store and reached for her bike. She was easing it out the door, walking backward, when someone tapped her shoulder. She looked to her left, felt a tap on her right, and looked that way. Still no one. Finally she turned around, coming face-to-face with a grinning Xander.

She punched him playfully in the arm. "Very funny! Jerk!"

He laughed, pulling her toward him with one arm. "I'm sorry. I was just playing with you." He dropped a quick kiss on her lips. "Where are you going?"

She followed his eyes to the bike, still balanced on one hand.

"Why?" she asked, hedging.

"My mom had a package for your dad. I was dropping it off when I saw you pulling out the bike. I thought we could get lunch or something."

"Actually, I just ate."

"Ah, okay." He hesitated. "So . . . where *are* you going?"

She thought about it. She hadn't really intended to tell anyone. But Xander was more than her boyfriend, however secret. He was also her friend.

She sighed, pulling the receipt from her shorts. "Last night when I was closing up the store, I found this."

He took it, looked at it for a few seconds, and handed it back. "I don't get it."

"It's a receipt."

"I can see that. So what?"

"I think that woman dropped it yesterday. The one who ordered the panther plasma."

"Wait a minute. You think this is her address?"

Claire nodded. "It's not the name of any of our regulars."

He rubbed his chin, his expression thoughtful. "Think you should give it to the Guild?"

She chewed her bottom lip. By the Guild, what he really meant was Estelle and Bernard Toussaint—his parents.

"I thought I might check it out first. You know, see if it's really her address?"

She held her breath, preparing herself for the argument Xander would give her. Instead, he opened his mouth to say something, seemed to think better of it, and closed it again.

"Want some company?"

FOUR

They took Xander's car from Claire's house in the University District all the way into the Quarter.

Xander turned onto one of the quieter streets that surrounded Washington Park. They had agreed it was best not to park right in front of the woman's house, and Xander pulled to a stop next to the curb on another small side street.

He turned to look at her. "Ready?"

She nodded and they got out of the car, looking up at the street signs as they went.

"I think it's up there," Xander said, pointing to the corner as they passed the park.

Despite the secrecy of their mission, Xander held her hand, staying on the outside of the sidewalk and generally doing everything possible to make Claire feel like a fragile female in need of protection. Asking him to stop wasn't an option. Xander's chivalry was bred as deeply in him as his belief in voodoo.

They stopped to check the address of the house on the corner against the receipt and did the same with the one across the street before deciding to take a right.

The houses were small and quaint, alternating between cute and slightly run-down. They saw a couple of "For Rent" signs as they continued down the street, the shade from the great oaks on either side providing welcome relief from the heat.

Claire made note of the house numbers as they walked. They were halfway down the block when she stopped.

"Wait . . ." She looked back at the iron gates they'd just passed. "I think that's it."

Xander tensed, scanning the gate for a house number and turning to Claire when he didn't find one. "How do you know?"

"Because the house back there is 546 and that one"— she pointed to the house on their left— "is 550. This one has to be 548, even though it's not marked."

"Okay," he agreed. "Now what? There's a court-yard."

Claire considered. The courtyards that fronted some of the city's homes made it impossible to get close without being spotted by someone inside the house.

"I don't know," she said. "Let's just wait. See if anyone comes or goes."

Xander sighed. "This is crazy. Even if we see the woman who came into the store yesterday, what will it prove? That she lives in New Orleans? She hasn't exactly made that a secret."

"I know, but—" Claire stopped, hearing the sound of heels on pavement. She pulled Xander behind the foliage of a large camellia bush.

They stood, bodies pressed together, trying to get a view of the sidewalk as the sound of footsteps grew louder. A few seconds later, the woman named Eugenia came into view. Her legs were long and slender in a black pencil skirt, a billowy white blouse over the top of it.

And she wasn't alone.

A man walked by her side. His head was bowed, silver hair glinting at his temples. He wore trousers and a snug button-down. A fraying rope bracelet was wound around his wrist, incongruous against the well-groomed backdrop of his clothing.

Claire sucked in her breath, a surge of energy pulsing through her skin at the sight of him. She shivered, the back of her neck growing slick with cold sweat, the blood running faster through her veins as panic set in.

Every instinct in her body screamed danger.

They watched as the pair stepped through the gate. It closed with a clang, and the footsteps suddenly stopped. The woman murmured, and Claire caught the sound of another voice, deeper and louder.

Xander glanced at her. She held a finger to her lips, listening, trying to catch snippets of the conversation between Eugenia, the man who'd arrived with her, and the third person she couldn't see.

A moment later, Eugenia and the silver-haired man resumed their progress toward the house, and a younger man stepped onto the sidewalk. Dressed in slim trousers and a fitted T-shirt, he walked right past Claire and Xander. His shoes, some kind of modern loafer, were quiet on the pavement. Claire tried to get a look at his face, but all she caught was a glimpse of pale skin, dark hair, and thin, angular features.

"That's it," Xander said when he was gone. "We're leaving."

Claire gazed over the bushes, eyeing the stucco building. "Maybe we should just—"

"No. We're leaving, Claire."

"You didn't even let me finish," she said angrily.

Xander crossed his hands over his chest. "You don't have to finish. I already know what you were going to say."

"How could you know when I didn't say it?"

"You were going to say we should have a look inside the courtyard."

Claire tried to cover her surprise. "Well . . . okay. That's what I was going to say. But so what? What harm will it do? Maybe we'll even get more information for the Guild."

Xander took her arm and began leading her away from the house. "I think the Guild can take it from here."

"Xander, just . . ." She tried to pull her arm from his grip, but he held tightly. She finally wrenched it free with an almost-painful tug. "Stop!"

He stopped walking. "What?"

"What's the matter with you?" she asked him, rubbing her arm. No one would ever accuse Xander Toussaint of being a wimp, but he wasn't a bully either.

Especially not with her. "Why are you acting like this?"

He took a deep breath. "Claire . . . you're just going to have to trust me. I don't know who these people are or what they're up to, but it's not good."

"How do you know that?" she asked. "You don't know any more than I do."

He shook his head. "I'm not doing this now. Let's go."

"You know something." She leaned against the trunk of an enormous oak. "And I'm not leaving until you tell me what it is."

Xander paced away from her before he turned back, defeat on his face. "You won't believe me anyway."

She thought about it. "Why? Because it has to do with voodoo?"

He hesitated before nodding.

"I promise I'll try to keep an open mind, okay? Now, spill."

He crossed the distance between them. "I had a dream last night. About you."

"Okay . . ."

"You were here, Claire," he said softly.

"What do you mean 'here'?"

"I mean, you were *here*. On this street. In front of this house."

She shook her head. "That doesn't make sense. Neither of us knew the woman lived here until now."

Xander's eyes didn't leave her face.

She sighed. "Lots of houses in the city look like this, Xander. You know that. And lots of streets look like this one, too. You could have been dreaming about anywhere."

His gaze still didn't waver. "It was *this* street. This house." He looked across the street at a red house with balconies on two levels. "That house was right where it is now. I even saw that beat-up car."

Claire's eyes settled on the old Chevy parked in front of the red house.

"Okay, so you dreamed about this. Maybe you have some kind of psychic ability or something."

"You believe in psychic ability but not in the craft?" he asked skeptically.

"They're totally different. One is based on superstition and the other . . ." She stopped. "Look, forget about it. Dreaming about us coming here doesn't mean something bad's going to happen."

"I didn't tell you the rest," he said softly.

She didn't want to hear it. She wanted to check out the house. See what they could find out about the woman and her friends. Most of all, she wanted to know how Eugenia knew her name when Claire had never seen her before in her life.

But Xander was shaken. Claire could see it in his eyes. He wasn't going to stay unless she heard him out.

She sighed. "Okay, tell me."

"It was dark, and you were being dragged out of the house, through that courtyard," Xander said, pointing to 548 Dauphine. "Then you were in a forest or a swamp or something. A Houngan priest was chanting and marking the area around you in a circle of blood. There was a fire burning and three other people in headdresses. The priest had a knife. He . . ." Xander stopped, his expression far away.

Claire knew that he wasn't making it up.

He was remembering.

"Keep going," she said, trying to keep her voice steady.

"He bled you. He cut open the veins in your forearms and bled you dry."

Claire couldn't speak. It wasn't just the dream. Everyone had dreams, even scary ones.

There was something else. Something familiar about the scene Xander had described. It was like she'd already lived it, even though she knew she hadn't.

She shook it off, reaching for his hand. "Look, it was just a dream, but if you want to go, we can."

He hesitated before pulling her to him. "I'm sorry, Claire. I just know you're not safe here."

She stood for a long time in the confines of his arms, trying to shake the feeling that he was right.

FIVE

Xander was silent as they headed across town. Claire spent the time thinking about the silver-haired man who had inspired such visceral fear. Who was he? And what did he and the others want with the panther blood?

When Xander finally spoke, Claire was surprised it wasn't about the people living in the house on Dauphine.

"We've been seeing each other for over a year now," he said.

"I know," she said quietly.

"I think it's time to get it out in the open, don't you?"

She looked out the window, trying to come up with something—anything—that wouldn't hurt him. Something that wouldn't sound like a repeat of everything she'd said before.

"I'm the last person your parents would want you to date," she finally said.

"This isn't about them." His voice was fierce. "It doesn't matter what they think."

She glanced back at him. "Maybe it matters to me."

He shook his head. "If it does, then your priorities are screwed up."

"It's not just your parents," she said. "Next year, you'll be at Duke or Emory, and I'll be . . . I don't know where, but—"

"Someplace far from here," he finished. "Probably cut off from the Guild like Crazy Eddie. I know. You've mentioned it once or twice."

She was taken aback by the bitterness in his voice. She'd known he was upset that she didn't want to go public with their relationship, but she didn't realize he was mad enough to compare her to Crazy Eddie, the only person Claire knew of who'd been kicked out of the Guild.

"I just don't see the point in pissing off your parents if we're going to be apart in a year anyway."

"Lots of couples stay together when they go to separate colleges," he said. "College isn't forever."

"You know it's more complicated than that," she protested.

"I guess I thought we were worth complicated," he said softly.

She stared at her hands, folded in her lap, not knowing what to say.

Sasha was waiting outside the yoga studio, her mat slung over one shoulder, when they pulled up to the curb. She had known about Claire and Xander almost from the beginning, and she watched as Xander hopped out to give Claire a quick, distracted kiss good-bye.

"See ya, Sash." He lifted his hand in a wave as he turned to go.

"Bye," she called back, turning to Claire. "Seriously, that guy gets hotter every time I see him."

Claire sighed. "Can we just go?"

Sasha looked surprised. "Sure," she said. "Everything okay?"

"It's . . . you know," Claire said. "Whatever. Let's just go. I could use some Downward Dog right now."

"Okay." Sasha looked at Claire's bag. "Where's your mat?"

"I had errands to do. I didn't want to haul it all over town. I'll borrow one from Cecile."

Vinyasa Yoga was on the second floor of an old building on Oak. Claire and Sasha climbed two flights of rickety stairs and entered the serene studio run by Cecile Rivera. They dropped their stuff and took a place on the floor as Cecile assumed her position at the front of the class. Sasha barely had time to tie back her braids before the session started.

For a while, Claire forgot everything about Eugenia Comaneci, the house on Dauphine, and her fight with Xander. Her body warmed and loosened a little more with each pose, her breathing deep and loud the way Cecile had taught her. By the time the hour-long session ended, Claire felt more stable.

She and Sasha were still lying on the floor in Corpse Pose when Sasha looked over at her. "Feel better?"

Claire smiled. "Much."

"Wanna go to the Cup?"

Claire nodded.

They got up, grabbed their stuff, and headed outside.

It was sticky and humid as they hurried down the street, anxious to get inside the air-conditioned haven of the Muddy Cup. They talked about the ball and the inevitable Guild gossip that would arise after a few hours with everyone in close proximity. A few minutes later, they entered the funky little coffee shop that was home to debates, study sessions, and the occasional heated argument.

After an hour with Cecile, Claire was feeling her lack

of lunch. She ordered a lemon blueberry muffin to have with her iced tea, and she and Sasha claimed their favorite table by the window.

"So? What's up? And don't say with what," Sasha said as soon as Claire set her bag down. "Because you know what I'm talking about."

Claire shook her head. "You know Xander. It's always the same thing."

Sasha took a sip of her coffee. Claire wondered how she always managed to drink it hot even when it was ninety degrees outside.

"Sure, I know Xander," she said. "But I know you, too."

"What's that supposed to mean?"

"Nothing. Just . . . Xander's a big picture kind of guy, and you're a detail person, that's all."

"What does that have to do with anything?" Claire broke off a piece of the muffin and put it in her mouth.

Sasha thought about it before answering. "It's like this: Xander loves you, and he knows you love him, right?"

"I guess . . ."

"Well, that's big picture stuff. For Xander, nothing else matters. He figures if you have that—the big stuff—the rest will work itself out. But all you see are the details. How will you date if you're going to college far away?

What if you stay together after college? How would you have a life together if he wants it to include the craft and you don't? Things like that."

"Yeah, but that stuff matters," Claire insisted. And then, the smallest shred of doubt. "Doesn't it?"

Sasha shrugged. "Depends on whether you think love or details are more important." Claire started to protest, and Sasha stopped her. "I'm not judging. I'm just saying. You can either work it out now or figure it out as you go. That part's up to you."

Claire watched people pass by on the other side of the window. She thought about Xander, about the tangled web that was their relationship, and the Guild and her lack of conviction next to his steadfast belief.

Whatever Sasha said, it wasn't as simple as she made it sound.

True love didn't always conquer all.

SIX

"We need to leave by twelve thirty today, Claire. Don't be late. I don't want to be rushed," her mother said at breakfast the next morning. She poured coffee into one of the delicate floral cups without spilling a drop.

Claire finished chewing her toast before she answered. "Twelve thirty?"

Her mother's expression turned to disbelief. "Hair and makeup? For the ball?"

"Oh, right."

The Priestesses' Ball was the highlight of the year for the Guild, a throwback to the past, when many members of New Orleans's high society were also secret practitioners of voodoo. Everyone in the Guild spent weeks running all over town in preparation, and her mother was no exception.

"Don't tell me you forgot!" her mother said. "After all that gown shopping?"

"Don't remind me," Claire groaned.

It had taken three weekends and eight different boutiques for Claire and her mother to agree on a dress. If she'd forgotten, it was only because of the order for panther blood and the receipt Claire had shoved into the top drawer of her desk after getting home from yoga yesterday. She was distracted, and who could blame her?

Her mother surveyed Claire with a mixture of sympathy and disappointment. "I thought shopping was fun. And besides, it was worth it. The gown is beautiful."

Claire fought a twinge of guilt. Her mom couldn't help who she was or how she'd been raised. And she was right; the dress was beautiful, just the right shade to bring out the green in Claire's hazel eyes.

Claire smiled. "Thanks, Mom."

"Did you give more thought to the headpiece?" her mother asked. "I can still pull some strings to come up with something simple."

"I don't need to give it more thought," Claire said. "I'm not wearing one."

The women of the Guild spent months planning elaborate headpieces to go with their gowns, often designing them to complement their family voodoo history. Claire hadn't worn a headpiece since she was too young to object to the ones her mother had forced on her.

Her mother was silent, trying to decide whether or not to press the issue.

Claire was relieved when she didn't say any more about it.

A few hours later, they made their way across town to Myrtle's, the scent of jasmine wafting around them as they stepped through the doors. Pilar wouldn't go any-where else, even in an emergency, preferring instead to wrap her hair in a fashionable scarf and wait for an ap-pointment. Claire would have liked to have tried one of the salons in the Quarter, but her mother wouldn't hear of it. And Claire had to admit that her own hair catas-trophes—including the time she'd tried to dye part of it blue only to have it turn a sickly and persistent shade of green—were always the result of experiments gone awry.

"Claire! And Pilar!" Myrtle was around the front desk even before they were all the way through the door. She put a hand on either side of Claire's face, the wrinkles deepening around her blue eyes as she smiled. "My! Look how you've grown. You've become a lovely young woman. Although" —she leaned back, her gaze becoming more critical— "I do think your hair is overdue some attention."

Claire just nodded and smiled. It was always easier that way.

Myrtle led them through the salon, chatting with Claire's mother about people they knew in common. They stopped at a station near the back.

"I booked you with Toni," Myrtle said. "As you know, she's the best when it comes to updos."

"I don't want an updo," Claire protested.

"Of course, you do." Her mother's voice was firm. "It's a formal event."

"So? Just because everyone else will have their hair piled on top of their head and plastered with two cans of hairspray doesn't mean I have to."

Her mother snapped her handbag closed with a tired sigh. "I wish you would be agreeable, Claire, just this once."

Claire was prevented from issuing a sarcastic retort when Toni emerged from the velvet curtains at the back of the salon.

"Hey, you two! You ready to knock 'em dead?"

Toni Moran was the only stylist at Myrtle's who was

under thirty. She was gorgeous, with porcelain skin and short red hair. Nearly five foot ten inches tall, with small, pixie-like features, she looked like she belonged on a catwalk in New York, not an old-school salon in the Garden District.

After a little discussion, they decided Claire would go first. Toni listened patiently while Pilar described the elaborate topknot she had in mind for Claire.

When her mother finished, Toni turned to Claire. "Is that what you want?"

Claire rolled her eyes. "Not exactly."

Toni cocked one hip, her mouth turning up at the corners. "Not exactly?"

"Okay," Claire said. "Not at all."

"Oh, Claire!" Her mother turned away in exasperation.

"How old are you now?" Toni asked.

"Seventeen."

"You're going to college next year, aren't you?"

Claire nodded.

"Then it's probably a good idea to start making these decisions yourself, wouldn't you say, Mrs. Kincaid?" Toni gestured to her chair without waiting for Claire's mom to answer. "Sit."

Claire did, and they discussed the options for her hair. At first, her mother said nothing, but after a while, she couldn't help herself. Finally, after a full-fledged negotiation, they agreed to meet in the middle and Toni went to work.

For the next forty-five minutes, Claire watched as Toni twisted pieces from the front, piling them onto her head bit by bit and pinning them in place. When she was done, Claire's hair still hung down her back, but the pieces from the front added volume to her crown. The effect was only slightly formal with a loose, effortless feel that allowed Claire to look at least a little like herself.

Claire looked at her mother in the mirror. Just because she'd agreed didn't mean she was going to be nice about it.

For a minute, no one said anything. Even Toni seemed to hold her breath until Pilar nodded, her lips curving into a smile. "You look beautiful, Claire. It suits you."

She returned her mother's smile in the mirror. "Thanks, Mom."

Easing herself out of the chair, she stepped aside as Toni wiped it down for Claire's mother.

"Let me just have Myrtle get someone for makeup . . ." Her mother turned toward the front desk.

"No makeup."

"Claire" —her mother tipped her head— "you can't go to the ball without makeup. It's a special occasion."

"I didn't mean I won't wear it," Claire protested. "I just don't want someone else to do it. I want to look like myself." She glanced over at Toni. "No offense."

Toni grinned. "None taken."

Her mother sighed deeply. "I suppose you're old enough to make your own decision about that, too." She favored Toni with a meaningful glare.

Claire smiled at the hairdresser in silent thanks.

Now that she was finished, Claire was itching to get out of the salon. It would take Toni at least an hour to touch up her mother's color. Add to that another forty-five minutes for the updo Claire knew her mom would want, and that left plenty of time for a walk and a few pictures. It took ten minutes of negotiating and a promise not to mess up her hair before her mother finally agreed.

Claire started up Jackson, her camera heavy in the bag hanging from her shoulder. She stopped at a neighborhood market for an apple and a candy bar, and hung a left on Coliseum Street.

She munched on the apple as she walked. The neighborhood had an ebb and flow, and she passed a few restored historical houses before crossing into a more rundown portion of the street.

Soon, the familiar white wall of the cemetery came into view. She walked alongside it, hanging a left on Washington. A couple of minutes later she came to the iron gates, LAFAYETTE CEMETERY emblazoned across the archway that marked its entrance.

Even as she stepped into the graveyard, she wasn't entirely sure why she was there. It had never been one of her favorite places, even when she wanted to take pictures. With its elaborate tombs of the city's most famous historical residents, it was too in-your-face, too obvious. The fact that a lot of the attention was due to its fame as the resting place for her great-great-grandmother just made it weirder.

Claire made her way through the aisles, marble tombs rising on either side. She could hear trumpets and trombones playing faintly in the distance. Other than that, it was unusually quiet.

She made her way past a tall white tomb, a red rosebush growing incongruously out of the tiny swath of grass in its shadow, and continued past the McClellan plot.

Eventually she came to the place she'd been heading for all along. For once, no one else was in front of the site, though there was the usual assortment of offerings left by strangers. Wilted flowers, half-burned candles, strings of beads, and a powdery residue whose composition Claire could only guess.

She lowered herself to the ground, leaning against the tomb, the marble cold against her back. She didn't know why she'd come. She'd decided long ago that her great-great-grandmother, like most legends, hadn't even resembled the portrait painted of her by history. At best, she was probably some half-baked, wannabe psychic.

At worst, a fake.

Claire thought absently of her camera and realized she had no desire to take pictures today. She took it out anyway and took a few shots of the tomb next to Marie's. A cheap plastic Virgin Mary figurine had tipped over on its side, and a half-crushed energy drink can lay crumpled on the ground in front of the marker. The composition was interesting, but Claire's heart wasn't in it. She put her camera away and pulled out the candy bar. Tearing it open and taking a bite, she thought about everything that had happened.

She and Xander hadn't talked about what to do next,

but she knew he would want her to fork over the receipt with Eugenia's address to the Guild. After that, they would take care of the woman and whatever plan she had for the panther blood, and Xander wouldn't dream about her being in danger again.

So why did Claire feel like something still had to be done? Like all at once, there was a ticking time bomb under her life that she couldn't ignore?

Polishing off the candy bar and stuffing the wrapper into her bag, she shook her head. She needed to get a grip, that's all.

When she stood up and checked her phone, she was relieved to see that it had only been an hour since she'd left Myrtle's. She was slipping it back into the pocket of her shorts when the tiny hairs on the back of her neck stood up.

Claire looked around. No one was there, but she couldn't shake the feeling that someone was watching her. She resisted the urge to break into a run and started walking.

She tried to hurry without seeming like she was afraid. She reached the entrance to the cemetery and hurried along the sidewalks, past the grand old homes, wanting nothing more than to get back to Jackson Street.

Ten minutes later, she did. She continued on toward Myrtle's, looking around one last time as she reached the door.

Her gaze was drawn to a man crossing the street. She knew who it was right away. It was more than his fitted slacks and the tight T-shirt, an almost-exact replica of what he'd been wearing yesterday when he'd left the house on Dauphine. It was the bend of his neck and the way she could tell, even behind the reflective lenses of his sunglasses, that he was watching her.

His head was turned in her direction, but he didn't seem concerned that she had seen him. It was unnerving, and as she pulled open the door to Myrtle's, she wondered if this was the first time she'd been followed.

SEVEN

The lights from the Toussaint house were visible even from the road. The ball itself wasn't a secret, but the purpose of the association that sponsored it—the Guild—was. Claire had once asked her mother about the neighbors. Didn't they wonder what was going on the one night a year when the Toussaints' was suddenly flooded with expensive cars, men in tuxedos, and women in gowns and feathered headpieces?

"New Orleans is overrun with historical societies and organizations, Claire," her mother had said, waving away the question. "No one cares about their purpose. People today don't want to know about the past."

It had surprised Claire, the idea that the Guild—as much a part of her everyday life as New Orleans itself—was something some people didn't even know or care about. That she was part of something so old that it was irrelevant, not only to her, but to everyone else, too.

Claire straightened the skirt of her dress. Guild events always made her nervous, and she'd spent the whole drive taking deep breaths, talking herself down.

They got out of the car, and her dad handed the keys to one of the jacketed men the Toussaints had hired to park cars. Claire's mother put on her headpiece. An elaborate creation of black feathers and faux amethyst with a silver band, it matched her deep blue gown perfectly. It had been too tall to fit on her head inside the car. Now she adjusted it while Claire's dad, dapper in his tuxedo, waited patiently and Claire held her bag.

Her mother turned to her, raising her eyebrows in question. "Good?"

Claire nodded. "Perfect."

"Is it even?"

Claire laughed. "It's even, it's even. Now let's go."

Her mother took her husband's arm and the threesome started up the walkway to the house.

The Toussaints had hired an older man to work the door, and he took their coats, handing them off to a woman standing at his elbow. Betsy was probably in the kitchen, watching the caterers with her infamous eagle eyes.

Claire trailed behind her mother and father, trying to fix a smile on her face as they headed down the hall, her emerald-green gown brushing against her bare legs.

A familiar blend of music grew louder as they approached the back of the house. Claire recognized the undercurrent of percussion—a distinctive beat that went hand in hand with many old-school voodoo rituals—coming from the soundproof walls of the ballroom while the strains of traditional New Orleans jazz came from the open doors leading to the back terrace. Estelle always had the music set up this way. As big as the Toussaint property was, the neighbors could probably still hear the music being played outside.

Better jazz than voodoo.

Claire stuck by her parents' side, the drumbeat vibrating under their feet as they crossed the threshold to the ballroom. It wasn't as big as the name suggested, but it did look beautiful, softly lit by the chandeliers that hung from the ceilings and the old-fashioned candle sconces that lined the walls. Tables were set up in a circle, the center of the floor kept clear for ritual dancing, and the room was decorated with elaborate floral arrangements combined with lush feathers. Everywhere Claire looked, headpieces caught her eyes, an explosion of colored feathers, jewels, and beads.

The room was packed with people she didn't recognize. While the Guild leadership was part of her everyday life, the Priestesses' Ball was one of the only times she saw the other Guild members, people who ran smaller stores throughout the South or wholesale supply houses online and were deemed important enough to receive a coveted invitation.

Percussionists played in the corner, and Claire's shoulders loosened a little with the beat. She didn't have to believe in voodoo to enjoy the music. It was a sound as familiar to Claire as her mother's voice. She'd probably heard it in the womb.

"Let's find a table," her mother said over the drums.

Claire wasn't surprised when she led them to a table at the front, near the dance floor. She might have been poor by birth, but Pilar Kincaid was no wallflower. She smiled and raised a hand in greeting to a few people as they passed.

Claire and her mother put down their bags while her father went to get them drinks. After taking a sip from the crystal goblet, Pilar announced that it was time to "mingle."

Claire nodded, but she had no intention of mingling. She just wanted to find Xander.

She made her way upstairs, looking for a quiet place where she could text him without seeming rude. She knew the Toussaint house as well as her own. Most of the Guild's big events were held there, and Claire had been roaming its halls since she was a kid.

She headed for the east wing, as far away from the staircase as possible. Her hopes were dashed that no one else would bother to go that far for a bathroom when she saw Allegra St. Martin in the hall, leaning toward an antique mirror and reapplying her lip stain. She wore a simple white dress that hugged her every curve. It stood in contrast to her exotic coloring and was topped off by an elaborate swan's feather headpiece, her glossy dark hair twisted up around it.

Feeling the twinge of self-consciousness that Allegra always inspired, Claire prepared to turn around and creep back the way she came.

"Hey," Allegra said, catching her eye in the mirror.

Claire sighed, continuing reluctantly toward the bathroom.

"Is someone in there?" Claire tipped her head at the closed door of the bathroom.

Allegra nodded, pulling back from the mirror. "Laura."

"I'll find another," Claire said, relieved for the excuse to leave.

Allegra's voice stopped her as she was turning around. "Claire."

"Yeah?"

Allegra bit her newly stained lower lip. "You're not as alone as you think, you know."

The words took Claire by surprise. She searched her mind, trying to figure out what Allegra was talking about. They weren't enemies. But they weren't friends, either.

"What do you mean?" she finally asked.

Allegra leaned against the ornate, gilded table under the mirror, one bare leg exposed in a slit that extended well above her knee. "Listen, I know you don't believe, but that doesn't mean the craft isn't real. And it doesn't mean you don't have the power, either. It's yours to call on whenever you need it."

"I really don't know what you're talking about," Claire said softly. But even as she said it, she was unnerved. Rumor was that Allegra had a proven gift for precognition and had predicted all kind of things—good and bad—since she'd been old enough to mix recipes and cast her own spells.

Allegra stepped toward her, stopping when they were only a foot apart. Claire flinched as the other girl put a gentle hand on her arm.

"You're in trouble," she said. "We all are."

"We?"

"The firstborns," Allegra clarified. Her eyes seemed to cloud over, her voice growing distant. "I can't see the threat clearly, but it's out there." She hesitated, seeming to return from some far-off place. "I know we've never been close, but I just wanted you to know that you're not alone. We're here for you, even if you don't want us to be." She smiled. "Kind of like family."

Claire was mesmerized by Allegra's eyes, an icy blue that stood in contrast to her Creole coloring, and a soothing quality in her voice that Claire had never noticed before. It took her a few seconds to step back and break the spell.

"Thanks. I appreciate the concern."

The door to the bathroom opened and Laura stepped out. She smiled in surprise.

"Claire! You look so pretty!"

Claire had to force herself to smile as she headed for

the bathroom. "Thank you. So do you." And she did, though Claire barely had time to register the black dress that set off Laura's shimmering copper hair as she made a beeline for the bathroom. "I'll catch up with you later."

She shut the door even before she turned on the light. Then she braced herself against the sink, taking big deep breaths and trying to resist the urge to puke. She told herself it was irrational. That Allegra was just drinking the voodoo Kool-Aid.

So why did she have a sinking feeling that Allegra was right? That something *was* coming for them—for her. That whatever it was had been put in motion by the order of the panther blood and the presence of the people on Dauphine.

Turning on the cold water, she used her hand to drink. She dried off her mouth with one of Estelle's fancy hand towels before fishing her phone out of her bag.

WHERE ARE YOU? she texted Xander.

ARBOR.

She left the bathroom, relieved to see that both Allegra and Laura were gone. The upper hallways were quiet, the noise from below growing louder as she came to the staircase.

When she reached the bottom of the stairs, she

worked her way through the crowd, leaving behind the rhythmic drumming and heading for the less insistent sounds of the jazz band in the backyard.

She was at the edge of the terrace when Sophie spotted her through the crowd. Her eyes lit up, and she ran toward Claire with a gap-toothed smile.

"Look, Claire!" She pointed to the empty spot on the top row of her teeth. "I lost a tooth!"

Claire laughed. "You definitely did! Did the tooth fairy leave you money?"

"Five dollars!" she exclaimed.

"What?" Claire feigned shock. "No way! You're totally treating next time we get ice cream."

Sophie beamed. She held out the skirt of her lavender dress, giving Claire a better look at the elaborate pleating. "Do you like my dress?"

"Love it," Claire said. She looked down at her own gown. "Do you like mine?"

Sophie nodded, grinning. She gestured for Claire to come closer and leaned in to whisper in her ear.

"You look beautiful. Xander will think so, too. He's waiting for you in the arbor."

Claire leaned back, unable to hold back her smile. "Thanks, kiddo. See you later."

Stepping off the terrace, she headed for the back of the property. It was just as beautiful outside as it was inside, the trees strung with white lights, multicolored lanterns hanging from their branches. Candles flickered on the tables that dotted the landscape, and torches were lit along the pathways that wound through the Toussaints' property.

Claire started down one of the paths and spotted Allegra huddled with Laura and the Valcours at one of the tables. Allegra smiled. Claire waved a hand in greeting, wondering if she'd stepped into some kind of alternate dimension where she and Allegra might actually be friends.

She continued toward the back of the property. The torches were more sparsely placed as she got farther away from the terrace, the night reaching out to her with inky fingers from the darkness beyond the path. She thought of the man who'd followed her to Layafette and picked up her pace, hurrying for the arbor and the safety of Xander's arms.

Two final torches marked the end of the path just in front of the arbor. Claire stepped into the shelter of a wooden structure that had been a meeting spot for the two of them since they first began their secret affair.

Candles were lit atop the iron table, white lights casting a golden glow from the wisteria vines above. She peered into the shadows.

"Xander?" She didn't know why she was whispering. There was no reason why she shouldn't be seen having a simple conversation with him. But the night seemed to hold its own secrets, and their meeting suddenly seemed like one of them. "You there?"

He stepped out of the darkness, and she sucked in her breath. She sometimes forgot how beautiful he was, but now, as he came toward her in his tuxedo, the candlelight flickering across his smooth skin, there was no denying it.

He pulled her into his arms, holding her for a minute before he leaned back to get a better look at her. His eyes roamed her hair and face, traveling the length of the green dress that skimmed her body in all the right places.

"You look stunning," he said.

She smiled. "Thank you. You don't look so bad yourself."

He narrowed his eyes, appraising her. She wondered if it was her imagination that there was a teasing glint in the upturn of his full mouth.

"I think you just need . . ." He turned around, heading for the table and pulling something from one of the chairs. "One more thing."

The box he handed her was large and flat. Wrapped in simple, glossy white paper, it was finished with an enormous green silk bow.

"What is this?" she asked, looking from the box to him. "It's for me?"

He nodded.

"Xander . . . You didn't have to get me something."

"Open it."

She took the box to the table and began removing the thick paper. "This is crazy." She lifted the lid. "You shouldn't have done this. I didn't get you anything."

"It's just a little something."

She peeled back the tissue paper inside the box, her eyes coming to rest on a garland of white peonies. "But . . . what is it?"

He reached around her, his body brushing hers as he lifted the item out of the box.

"You don't have to wear it if you don't want to," he said. "I know you don't like headpieces. It just . . ." He cleared his throat. "It's different. It made me think of you."

He held the headpiece up. The white peonies were open and lush, wound with peacock feathers that came to an exotic point in the front, a large jewel, as green as her dress, dangling like a teardrop. Green ribbon in more shades than she could count trailed off the back of it. It was almost casual, breathtaking in its understatement.

"Xander . . ." Tears stung her eyes. This was just like him. To give her something that celebrated both her individuality and the heritage she couldn't seem to deny. "If I'd known a headpiece could so beautiful, I would have chosen it myself."

"You like it?"

"Like it?" She threw her arms around his neck. "I love it. Thank you."

He peeled her arms away and placed the headpiece on her head, adjusting it a couple of times before he slid in the combs that were built into the sides to hold it in place. When it was secure, the emerald rested against her forehead, the ribbons trailing through the curls down her back.

"How does it look?" she asked.

"Almost as gorgeous as you." His voice was low, his eyes hooded with a desire Claire recognized from the times they got a little too carried away.

She smiled, but it only lasted a second. "Wait . . . What am I going to tell my parents?"

The light seemed to drop from his eyes, his jaw tensing. "I've taken care of it. Sophie helped me pick it out. She'll say it's a gift from her. No one will question it. She's always adored you."

Claire stepped toward him, regret clogging her throat, making it difficult to speak.

She touched his shoulder. "I'm sorry. I didn't mean to . . ."

"It's fine."

"You know I love you."

His laugh was bitter. "In secret?"

She swallowed hard. "I know how it sounds, but I'm protecting you as much as myself."

He ran a hand through his hair, turning away. "Right."

Claire searched for something to say. Something that would make him understand. That would bring back the magic of the moment before she'd reminded him that their differences were still there, just as glaring as they always were.

Then, the murmur of voices caught the air through the distant sounds of the band playing on the terrace. It was different from the conversation and laughter of the guests sitting at the outdoor tables. This was the sound of two people arguing but trying to keep their voices down.

And it was coming from behind the carriage house, just beyond the arbor.

Xander's gaze met hers, a silent question in his eyes. She slipped off her shoes in answer and moved past him, out of the arbor.

They stepped carefully across the gravel pathway, the tiny rocks digging into the tender bottoms of Claire's bare feet. The voices grew louder as they approached the big doors of the carriage house.

Continuing past the front of the old building, they stepped onto the grass that ran along one side, stopping when they came to the end of the structure.

The voices were louder now. Claire could hear some of what was being said, first by a man, his voice a low rumble, and then by a feminine one Claire recognized.

She swiveled her head to look at Xander, wondering if he recognized it, too. She could see in his eyes that he did.

And he should. Because it was the voice of his mother.

EIGHT

"The Guild wasn't there when I needed it," the man said. "And neither were you. Did you . . . accountable?"

Estelle Toussaint's voice whispered. "I'm sorry . . . the rules, Max."

Claire tried to piece together the snippets of conversation, drifting like smoke through the night. She leaned forward, peering around the side of the building. She felt Xander's body against her back, his breath near her ear, and knew that he was looking, too.

It took a minute for her eyes to adjust to the darkness. At first, she continued to hear pieces of conversation, but couldn't find their source. Then, she made out a faint gray smudge near the trees behind the carriage house. She blinked a couple of times, willing her eyesight to sharpen.

It was Estelle all right, her silver gown a shimmery

column in the darkness, just as Claire had thought. But as surprising as it was to see Xander's mother having a secretive conversation behind the carriage house while her guests attended the ball, the identity of her companion was even more shocking.

Claire would have sworn it was the older man from Dauphine Street, the one who had arrived in the company of Eugenia Comaneci. True, it was dark. But there was something familiar about the tip of his head, the harsh set of his mouth. His chiseled jaw visible even in profile.

And that wasn't all. Even as she tried to make out his features through the shadows, cold sweat sprang to her forehead. A wave of nausea hit her as the same dark energy she'd felt on Dauphine reached out from where the man stood.

When she dropped her eyes to his wrist, she was sure. The rope bracelet was there, the glint of a silver bead visible in the moonlight.

She looked back, her eyes meeting Xander's shocked stare, still locked on his mother and the mysterious man.

"You are . . . treading on dangerous . . ." Estelle said, her voice a low hiss. "The Guild . . ."

"The Guild is a worthless group of entitled hacks so

far removed from the origins of the craft that they can do little more than light candles and mix herbs. You're more concerned with . . . and parties than . . . the craft for that which it was intended." Even broken up as they were, his words were a condemnation, not only of their parents, but of all of them. Claire felt it like a punch to the stomach. "I'm not afraid of . . . I'm no longer under your control. You saw to that a . . . time ago."

"Everything . . . this matter is under our control. If you don't know that yet, you have a lot to learn, even after all this time."

The man grabbed her arm as she turned to go. Xander's body tensed. Claire had no doubt that if the man made one more move toward Estelle, Xander would be all over him.

"You mete out . . . as if there will never be consequences. It's time for you to be on the other side of the equation," the man said, his face mere inches from Estelle's. "Don't make the mistake of thinking our previous . . . buys you any consideration now."

They stood like that, their eyes locked, for a few seconds before Estelle wrenched free, rubbing the place where his hand had gripped her arm.

She turned around, marching straight toward Claire

and Xander. They flattened themselves against the building. trying not to breathe as she made her way past them. When she was gone, Claire leaned forward, peering at the place where Estelle had stood with the man, wondering if he had left, too.

But he was still there, staring in her direction.

Xander tugged on her hand, pulling her back toward the arbor.

Claire stumbled. "Xander . . . wait!"

He looked down at her as he propelled them over the pathway. "We can talk in a minute. I don't want you anywhere near that guy."

They exited the pathway onto a stretch of grass. The torches lit around the yard combined with the music to create a festive air. It was hard to believe just a couple of minutes before they'd been witness to what had seemed very much like a threat.

And maybe even a reference to some kind of affair.

"Champagne?"

Xander looked at the man standing at his shoulder, then took one, tipping his head and downing the liquid in one gulp before setting the empty glass back on the tray.

Claire touched his arm. "Are you okay?"

She had never seen him lose his cool. Not once in all the time she'd known him. The only time she'd even seen him upset was the few times they argued about whether or not to come clean with their relationship.

He shook his head. "Who was that? And why was he talking to my mother that way?"

Claire pulled him to the side. Several people at Allegra's table glanced their way. "You know who it was. It was the man from Dauphine Street."

He shook his head, his jaw set in a hard line of denial. "We can't be sure of that. It was dark. It could have been anybody."

"It was him," she insisted. "He was wearing the same bracelet. He had the same face."

"There's probably more than one bracelet like that in the city, Claire. And we only got a quick look at the side of his face when we were spying on that house yesterday."

She wanted to argue. To prove her point. But looking at Xander's face, at the combination of anger and confusion in his eyes, she didn't have the heart.

She took Xander's hand. "You're probably right."

و ل

The rest of the night was tame compared to the beginning. They met up with Sasha and took advantage of the party by heaping their plates full of traditional New Orleans food, including delicious doughy beignets, almost invisible under heaps of powdered sugar. Later, she and Xander shared a few dances, and they ended up with a bigger group that included Allegra, Laura, and Charlie and William Valcour. Claire was surprised to find that she was actually having fun.

Xander went through the motions, but she could see the strain on his face. Every now and then, she caught him looking at his mother. Claire wondered if it was her imagination that Estelle looked flustered and distracted.

The crowd started disbursing around midnight. Claire managed a semiprivate good-bye with Xander in the shadow of the big magnolia tree at the side of the Toussaint house before she met up with her parents to leave. Then she was removing the headpiece from her hair and leaning back against the leather seat of the Lexus as her dad drove them home and her mother talked nonstop about everything that had happened at the ball and everyone who was there.

"That was so lovely of Sophie to get you the headpiece, wasn't it, Claire?" her mother said, twisting in the front seat to look at her.

"Hmm-mmm." Claire tried to smile, but the flush

of contentment she'd felt only moments before was dimmed by the reminder that she'd hurt Xander.

Again.

That she was hurting him even now as she denied the gift was from him.

ஜ

The next morning, she dragged herself out of bed and took a quick shower, dressing in shorts and a tank top before heading downstairs for her shift in the store.

They'd received a new shipment of supplies from the Caribbean, and Claire spent the morning cross-referencing the items in the boxes against the Kincaids' purchase order forms and the packing slips from the wholesaler. Documentation from their suppliers was always sketchy, usually handwritten instead of printed on a computer, and it took Claire most of the morning to decipher the almost-illegible script.

Once all the paperwork was in order, Claire began unpacking everything, transferring it into the glass jars, canisters, and tins the Kincaids used to store ingredients on their shelves. The time passed quickly, her thoughts flitting from Xander's disappointment in her to the conversation they'd overheard between Estelle and the stranger behind the carriage house.

If the man was involved in the requisition for pan-ther blood, why was Estelle talking to him? And if the Guild had already identified him as the man behind the order, why had Estelle spoken to him in private instead of bringing him before the rest of the Guild leadership?

She'd just unpacked the last item and was breaking down the shipping boxes for recycling when the private door opened. Xander stepped into the store, closing the door behind him. He put his hands in the pockets of his jeans and looked at her.

"So," he finally said. "Want to check out that house on Dauphine again?"

NINE

Xander was quiet as they drove across town. Claire didn't press him. She could only imagine the possibilities running through his mind.

They found a spot on the same street they'd parked on two days earlier.

Xander turned to her. "So what, exactly, is the plan?"

She'd been thinking about it ever since he agreed to go with her. "I think we should case the place, do our best to make sure the house is empty, and then try and get past the courtyard." It wasn't exactly foolproof, but it was the only thing Claire could think of.

"Then what?" Xander asked.

"We break in," she said. "See what we can find."

Xander took a deep breath. "Maybe you should go home. Let me see what I can find out on my own."

Claire shook her head. "No way. I'm not letting you go in there alone."

"Claire, I don't want you to get hurt because I need to find out what my mom was doing with that guy."

She folded her arms across her chest. "This isn't just about your mom. In case you forgot, these people came into our store, too, and Eugenia knew my name."

Xander considered, finally nodding in agreement. "Okay. But if I even smell trouble, we leave. No questions asked, okay?"

Claire agreed. It's not like she wanted to get caught breaking and entering.

They got out of the car and headed down Dauphine, slowing when the camellia bush came into view. Resuming their positions from the first time they'd staked out the house, Claire peered through the bush, focusing in on the courtyard.

"Let's just wait," Xander said. "See if anyone comes or goes before we take a chance with the courtyard."

Claire nodded. She took advantage of the time by taking in as much detail as she could about the layout of the courtyard and house, noting where the windows and doors were and where the landscaping might give them some cover.

The entire courtyard was lined with large, overgrown bushes. If they stayed near the walls, no one would see them coming.

That was the good news.

The bad news was that there weren't very many ways in, at least from the front.

Claire turned to Xander. "Let's get closer, check it out."

"Wait." He put a hand on her arm to stop her. "How do we know no one's home?"

"We don't," Claire conceded. "But there's only one way to find out."

Xander hesitated before nodding. "Okay, but if someone's there, we leave. And I don't think we should go in through the front gate."

Claire scanned the courtyard. The ocher-colored house sat between two others, separated by a tall iron fence on one side and a slightly lower stucco wall on the other.

"We could try to get over that wall."

He followed her gaze. "Can you do it?"

She rolled her eyes. "You mean because I'm a girl?"

"No," he said, with a sigh. "Because you're short."

"Oh." Now she felt stupid. "I don't know, but I can try."

Xander was already heading for the other side of the stucco wall. The house on that side was small and poorly maintained, set back from the street and shrouded in the low-hanging branches of a giant oak tree.

They eased into the neighbor's yard, helped along by the leafy shrubs and bushes that grew along the side of the little house. Staying undercover while edging along the stucco wall, they continued toward the back of the property until a sound from inside the house brought them to a stop. They looked at one of the shack's windows, where the flickering light of a TV, the source of the noise, cast shadows on the yellowing, lace curtains.

Locking eyes, they stood silently for a few seconds before continuing to the back of the house.

The backyard was even worse than the front, the grass dry and scraggly, dirt showing through in patches. A dog on the other side of the back fence barked ferociously.

"Hurry," Xander whispered. "That dog's blowing our cover."

He bent to one knee, lacing his fingers together and cupping his hands.

Claire slipped off her flip-flops and stuffed them into

the waistband of her shorts. She placed her bare foot in Xander's hands.

"One . . . two . . . three," he whispered.

Her knee buckled a little as he lifted her into the air. She touched the wall with one hand, using it to steady herself on the way up. When she was almost level with the top, she grabbed for it with both hands. She hung there for a few seconds, the wall under her arms, before she was able to pull herself upright and turn to a sitting position.

She looked down at Xander. "Want me to give you a hand?"

He shook his head. "But stay there until I'm up and over. I don't want you in the courtyard alone."

She didn't know whether to be annoyed or grateful by his overprotectiveness. But the dog was still barking, and somewhere in the yard behind them a screen door opened with a creak and then slammed shut as someone stepped outside, cursing at the dog. Claire scooted over so Xander would have enough room to heave himself up and over.

He eyed the wall, seeming to gauge the distance between it and where he stood on the ground. Then he took two steps back and sprinted toward it, jumping at the last second and grabbing onto the wall with both hands. Some of the stucco broke loose, crumbling to the ground with a soft patter.

Xander only hung there for a second, the muscles in his brown arms flexing under his white T-shirt as he pulled himself up, his stomach resting on the wall. He bent one knee, using it as leverage to get on top of the wall. Then he swung both legs over and dropped to the ground on the other side.

Claire spun around, watching Xander scan the courtyard.

"All clear," he whispered, looking up at her. "Can you jump?"

She nodded, and he stepped back to give her room. She landed with a soft thud on the gravel that lined each side of the courtyard.

Xander gestured toward the back of the house. Claire followed, sticking as close to the stucco wall as the bushes would allow. There were a couple of small windows on the side of the house, but they were covered by draperies. Not ideal. If they cased the house through a curtained window and someone was on the other side, they wouldn't know until it was too late.

They kept going, stopping at the end of the house

to make sure nobody was in the backyard. When they were sure it was empty, they eased around the corner.

The back had more opportunities for entry. There was a bank of French doors plus a balcony on the second floor that ran the length of the house.

Xander looked back at Claire. "What now?"

"I don't know," Claire admitted. "Try the doors?"

"They're glass. What if someone's in the room?"

"We could try the other side," she suggested.

"Okay, but stay behind me and be ready to run if someone's home."

Claire followed him around the corner, and they were immediately engulfed in shade, giant trees blocking out the heat and sun. Panic clutched at her chest as they made their way along the narrow walk between the house and the fence. The possibilities were slim for escaping such a tight spot in a hurry.

Xander continued to the first window. It was open. Not by much, just an inch at the bottom, but it was better than nothing.

Claire nodded when he pointed to it.

He stood on tiptoe, peering inside. Then he slid the window upward. A rush of hot air escaped the room.

He turned to her. "If there's trouble, you go. You can

get help if you want, but you have to promise to go."

She nodded. There was no way she'd leave him behind, but he wouldn't keep going if she didn't agree.

He hoisted himself up onto the windowsill, swinging his legs in so gracefully he could have been a gymnast. His head appeared in the window frame a few seconds later.

"So far so good. Want me to check it out first?"

She shook her head. "No way."

He sighed. "Okay. Need help?"

"No." She was already reaching for the sill. After the stucco wall, the window was no problem. She pulled herself up and slid into the room as if she were exiting the deep end of a pool without a ladder.

Then she was inside, looking around and taking stock of her surroundings.

TEN

They were in a mudroom. The air was heavy and hot, the sound of water rushing in the washer and clothes tumbling in the dryer coming from the corner of the room. No wonder the window had been left open a crack. It was hotter than Hades, as Claire's mother would say.

Xander crept to the door, leaning out just enough to see the rooms beyond. Claire stayed near his back, trying to restrain her own desire to look while she waited for the all clear.

He turned around, his eyes meeting hers. "Stay close."

She followed him into a long hallway, the wooden floors partially covered by a long exotic-looking runner. It was quiet, with no sign that anyone was home. To the back of the house, Claire could make out a round table and what was probably a kitchen and dining area that opened onto the patio at the back of the house.

"Be right back," Xander whispered, heading for the room at the back of the house. He returned a moment later. "All clear in there, too."

They followed the hall toward the front of the house. There was a powder room on the left and a staircase leading to the second floor on the right. They continued past both to a small, high-ceilinged room that stood to one side of the entry. It had probably been a parlor at some point, but now it looked like a living room. A sofa stood in the middle of the room and was flanked by two chairs. A wooden coffee table punctuated the center of the sitting area.

Something about the room felt off to Claire. It took her a minute to figure it out. The house felt dead. It was like a hotel room, pleasant and clean but with no sign of life. Even the decor was bland and impersonal. She seriously doubted they would find anything incriminating.

She caught Xander's eye and headed toward the stairs.

The made their way slowly up the staircase. Claire was used to living in an old house, and she tested each tread before taking a step, wanting to make sure it wouldn't creak. They couldn't know the house was empty until they'd checked all the rooms, and her heart beat a mile a minute, her body prepared to run as they ascended to a generous landing.

There were five rooms on the second floor, two of them with closed doors. Claire was willing to bet they were empty. The air was too still, the atmosphere devoid of life. She stepped toward the open doors first, peeking inside each before she lost her nerve.

No one was there, and she breathed a sigh of relief as she took in the two standard-issue bedrooms, each of them holding a bed, bureau, desk, and chair.

The third open door was a bathroom. She left it alone. No one hid anything important in the bathroom.

She looked at Xander, raising her eyebrows in silent question and pointing to one of the closed doors.

He nodded, and she stepped toward the first room.

She eased the door open carefully, wincing when it creaked. Despite her belief that no one was in the house, she was relieved when an empty room was revealed.

This was where Eugenia slept, Claire was sure of it. The ghost of a heavy, classical perfume hung in the air; a set of elegant luggage stood against the wall. An iron banister was visible through a pair of French doors. Claire guessed it was the balcony at the back of the house.

Just to be safe, she turned and pushed open the door to the final room. Empty.

"No one's home," she said to Xander, tipping her head to the room that had been behind the first closed door. "I'm going to check out this one. Want to take the first two?"

He nodded. "We'll do the last one together since it fronts the street. That way, one of us can keep watch."

He disappeared through one of the doorways and Claire stepped into Eugenia's room, her eyes coming to rest on a desk near the glass doors.

Something was tacked to the wall in front of it.

Stepping toward it, she stopped when she saw what was on its surface. She leaned in to get a better look at the photograph staring back at her.

It was a picture of Xander, walking one of the city's streets, his hands shoved carelessly in his pockets. Claire recognized the blur of storefronts behind him. Probably somewhere near her house, though she couldn't be sure. Xander, obviously the target of the photograph, took up almost the whole frame.

Claire's heart thudded in her chest as her eyes surveyed the wall around Xander's picture.

His wasn't the only one. There was a photo of Charlie

and William Valcour, sitting side by side at an outdoor café.

But this one was different; a red X was drawn through it.

The next picture was of Allegra St. Martin. Even through the red X, Claire could tell Allegra was in her car. Her black hair was shiny and full, her arm resting on the open window frame as she sat in the driver's seat, probably stopped at a red light or something.

She thought of Allegra at the ball, how unexpectedly nice she'd been, and a chill ran up Claire's spine.

"What the . . ." Xander said behind her, leaning over her shoulder. "What is all this?"

Claire was both mesmerized and horrified by the images in front of her. "I don't know."

The next picture was of Laura, a lock of curly hair falling forward as she bent her head to a book. The photo was crossed through with a red X just like the others.

Next to Laura's picture was a photograph of little Daniel, walking next to someone much taller as he ate a dripping ice-cream cone. His picture had an X, too.

There was only one more image, tacked next to Daniel's. Claire's heart almost stopped when she saw Sasha's smile, brilliant even in the black-and-white photo, the strap of her yoga mat just visible on one shoulder. Claire didn't know whether to be relieved or scared that Sasha's photo, like Xander's, lacked the red X.

Her eyes roved the photographs, trying to figure out why the woman named Eugenia would have photographs of all of the young Guild members.

No. Not all.

All of the oldest children of the Guild's most prominent families were represented on the wall—except for Claire.

"I don't know what this is," Xander said, "but we should hurry if we're going to check out the other room. We've been inside for almost half an hour, and we have no idea how long they've already been gone and when they'll be back."

Claire nodded, pulling out her phone and taking a quick picture. The sight of the wall covered with photos—photos of people she knew and loved—was undeniably disturbing.

She glanced around, wanting to make sure they weren't missing anything obvious, as they headed for the hall.

As soon as they entered the final room, Claire guessed it was Max's. The furnishings were just as generically antique as everywhere else in the house. A leather valise sat on top of the desk under the window and the heavy draperies were pulled shut as if to block out the modern world.

But it was more than that. The air was heavy with something bleak and dangerous. A palpable darkness, an ominous vibration she could feel under her skin. She had to fight the urge to run from the room. Fight the need to escape the feeling that something evil was wrapping its fingers around her heart and soul.

"One of us should keep watch while the other searches," Xander suggested.

Claire forced herself to focus. "Want to take guard duty while I keep searching?"

"Sure." Xander moved to the side of the desk and took up residence near the window.

The desk was the most obvious place to start. It was old, probably rented with the house. The wood was dark, its grain coarse and visible even under the papers, files, and valise that cluttered its top.

Claire started with the top drawer. She didn't know what she expected, but it wasn't complete emptiness. It didn't even hold a pen or a paper clip.

She moved onto the drawers on either side of the footwell. They were empty, too, except for a stack of printer paper on the left.

She looked up at Xander. "Anything?"

He shook his head, eyes still on the street, and Claire turned her attention back to the desk.

The first thing that caught her eye was the corner of a photograph, peeking out from behind the folders and papers that littered the top of the desk.

This one was different from the ones on the wall in Eugenia's room. Older. It showed a group of people standing on a lawn somewhere. It looked like a party. The adults held glasses in their hands and the children were dressed for some kind of important occasion. There was something vaguely familiar about it, but Claire couldn't put her finger on what it was.

She set it aside and moved on to the file folders on top of the desk.

The first one held travel information, including itineraries and flight plans from Romania to Paris and then to New York. It didn't surprise her that Eugenia and her companions were foreign, though Claire hadn't expected Romania. Her eyes ran down the list of names: Eugenia Comaneci, Maximilian Constantin, Jean-Philip Constantin, Herve Constantin.

Maximilian Constantin. Max. The silver-haired man Estelle Toussaint had been talking to near the carriage house. And who were Jean-Philip and Herve? Maximilian's sons?

She filed the questions away in her mind. Whoever they were, there weren't three of them as she and Xander had thought—there were four.

Which meant one more possibility of someone stumbling on them in the house.

She picked up her pace, moving the first file aside and opening the one underneath it to reveal a stack of paper.

She flipped through it, trying to get her head around what it was.

"Xander . . ." she said softly.

He looked over at her.

"It's a list of all the Guild's supply houses in the city." She paged to the back of the stack, her hands slowing. "Scratch that. It's a list of all the Guild's supply houses."

"All of them where?" Xander asked.

Claire shook her head. "Everywhere. Here, the rest of the United States; there are even addresses in London and Asia and . . . here's one in Turkey."

Xander thought about it. "Well, Eugenia does have a key. I guess we shouldn't be surprised that they have a list of our locations. They're entitled to entry anywhere."

"I guess," she murmured, looking at all the names and addresses. She hadn't realized the Guild was so far-reaching. "But why would they need a list in every country?"

"I don't know, but I think we should hurry." He turned back to the window and parted the draperies.

Claire closed the file. She shuffled through the rest of the papers on the desk, but there was nothing more of interest. Just some receipts for area restaurants, a streetcar ticket, and strangely, a movie stub.

Claire focused on the valise. It was substantial and masculine. She could almost see the man named Maximilian moving through the city, the leather case under his arm.

She undid the brass clasp and folded back the top, surprised at how thick and supple the leather was. The case had to be old. Really old.

She put her hand inside and felt around. Her fingers brushed against several objects and came to rest on some kind of booklet. She removed it from the case.

It was Maximilian's passport, and it was loaded with stamps. Germany, France, Hungary, China, the Caribbean, even Cuba. He had been everywhere, the dates spread out over the last few years.

She set it aside and reached back into the valise, withdrawing a long, flat piece of leather, tied with cord. Something was inside it. She unlaced the cord, unrolling the leather case on top of the desk until it lay flat, revealing a stack of folded papers.

She lifted it out of the case, releasing an odd, almost unpleasant scent. Mildew, firewood, and a bitter tang that might have been a residue of the old leather.

Unfolding the stack, she skimmed over the first page. It was yellowing, dry and thin in her fingers, the edges uneven. Formatted like a letter, it appeared to have some kind of greeting at the top (*Le Plus Chere Sorina . . .*) and paragraphs underneath it.

There was just one problem; it was entirely in French.

She let out a frustrated sigh.

Xander looked up from the window. "What is it?"

She started paging through the stack. "They look like letters, but they're in—" She stopped, her eyes skimming the rest of the pages. "Wait a minute . . ."

"What's going on?"

"I thought they were in French, but some of them are in English."

He held out a hand. "Let me see."

She passed them to him.

His eyes roamed the pages. "The English pages are translations, I think."

"How do you know?" she asked. "You don't speak French."

He glanced at the window before leaning toward her.

"I know, but look . . ." He held out the first page. "'*Le Plus Chere Sorina*.'"

Then he pointed to the second page's greeting.

"'My dearest Sorina,'" Claire murmured, reading the small, slanted script.

Xander was right; they were the same. Someone had already translated the letters.

He looked back at the window. "We need to hurry."

"I know. I'm trying."

She skimmed the English version, words and phrases jumped out at her as she read.

. . . the darker parts of our art . . .

. . . your questions about black magic . . .

. . . possible to curse someone . . .

Turning the paper over, her eyes were pulled to the signature at the bottom of the page. "What the . . . ?" Her voice was a whisper.

"What now?" Xander asked.

She pointed to the looping scrawl. "Look."

His eyes met hers. "Marie Leveau?"

Claire looked back at it, wanting to be sure. But she knew that signature. Had seen it in the family spell and ritual book.

"That's what it says. And look." She pointed to the date on the front. "Eighteen eighty. Which means they were probably from Marie the First, not her daughter." Claire shook her head. "Why would these people have letters from my great-great-grandmother?"

Xander pulled his eyes reluctantly from the pages to look back at the street. "I don't know, but we need to wrap it up."

"Why? Is someone coming?"

"Not yet." He checked his phone again. "But we've been here too long already. I don't want to push our luck."

He was putting his phone back in his jeans when Claire got an idea. She laid all the letters flat on the desk and took out her phone.

"What are you doing?" Xander asked.

"I'm taking pictures so we can get a better look at these later."

He didn't say anything, but she knew he was stressing. She saw it in the tense set of his shoulders and the way he rubbed his hand against the barely there whiskers on his chin as he looked at the street.

She tried to hurry, taking pictures of each letter and putting them back in place, careful to keep them in the order she'd found them. When she was done, she snapped a picture of the group photograph just for good measure.

She put the letters back inside the leather case and returned everything to the valise. Her fingers brushed against a small, cold object. Taking a hold of it, she removed it from the leather case.

It was a glass vial, full of red liquid. There was a paper label stuck to it, and Claire lifted it to her eyes, trying to read the script.

She read it three times, shaking her head in disbelief, before she was sure.

"You're not going to believe this," she murmured.

"We have to go," Xander said suddenly. "Right now."

Claire looked up. "Why?"

"A black Range Rover just pulled up outside."

ELEVEN

Xander pulled her toward the door.

"Wait!" She struggled against him, freeing herself from his grip.

She ran back to the desk, looking it over, trying to remember where everything was when they'd entered the room. Slipping the vial back into the leather valise, she folded the flap down and latched it closed. Then she took a quick pass at the papers and files on the desk, straightening them until they seemed to be in place.

"Which way out?" she asked as she followed Xander out of the room.

"Not through the front."

The sound of a key being inserted into a lock came from the front door.

"They're coming!" Claire said.

"This way." Xander grabbed her hand, pulling her toward Eugenia's room.

He headed straight for the balcony, parting the curtains and opening one of the glass doors.

"Xander . . ." Dread built inside Claire as she realized what he was thinking. "There aren't any stairs leading down from the balcony."

He was already stepping outside when he met her eyes. "I know, but we don't have a choice. I'll help you down."

The door opened in the foyer below, and the sound of voices drifted up the stairs.

Claire stepped out onto the balcony with Xander.

"How are we going to do this?" she asked, looking down. The ground seemed a lot farther away from the balcony than the balcony had seemed from the ground.

"I'll go down first. I hate leaving you up here, but I don't want to send you down without me, in case someone's in the kitchen." He took a quick look down. "I'll catch you when you drop."

She didn't doubt for a second that he would. "What about you?"

His face was grim. "Don't worry about me."

Then he was stepping over the railing, hanging precariously in midair as he bent to grab hold of the banister. When he had both hands wrapped around the iron at the bottom, he let his body drop. The iron creaked as he swung.

The voices grew louder as they moved up the stairs to the second floor of the house.

Claire leaned over the railing. "They're on the stairs!"

He let go, landing on the stone with a muffled groan and stumbling before he got his footing.

He was under the balcony a second later. "Do what I did, and I'll catch you."

She was stepping over the railing when Eugenia burst into the room. She surveyed Claire with total calm, the serene expression never wavering from her face.

"We have company," she called to someone behind her.

Eugenia locked eyes with Claire as she stepped over the railing.

"Now!" Xander instructed. "I've got you!"

She forced herself not to look. She didn't have time to be afraid. She released her hold on the banister, her stomach still somewhere up by the balcony as she fell toward the ground.

Then Xander's arms were around her. She had only a

moment to be relieved before he grabbed her hand and ran.

"They're heading for the side of the house. Get them," Eugenia commanded from the balcony.

They rounded the corner of the house, but this time, Xander didn't bother with the stucco wall. Stealth didn't matter anymore. Now it was all about escape.

They hit the front of the property. Two men were heading into the pathway at the other side of the house. Claire recognized one of them as the guy who'd followed her to the cemetery. She hadn't seen the other one before, but she guessed that together they were Jean-Philip and Herve Constantin.

They stopped, their eyes fixed on Xander and Claire in surprise. It was only a second, but it was enough. Xander pulled her toward the front gate, flinging it open and practically throwing her onto the sidewalk.

They were running again, this time down the street, putting as much distance between them and the house as they could.

Claire didn't dare glance back until they reached the corner. She expected to see the men on their heels, or at the very least, staring after them from the sidewalk in front of the house. There was no one there.

It wasn't until later, when she and Xander were a safe distance away, that she realized why they hadn't been followed. The men didn't need to chase them.

They already knew where Claire and Xander lived.

☙

"Why would they place three orders for panther plasma if they already have some?" Claire asked. "Black magic doesn't usually call for that much of one ingredient."

They were sitting in Xander's car, parked around the block from Claire's house.

Xander shook his head. "I don't know, but there's something I didn't get to tell you."

"What?"

"When I went to the kitchen, there was a map spread out on the table."

"A map? Of what?" she asked.

"Head of Island."

"Head of Island?" She'd driven past the area with her dad once on the way to pick up supplies from another store. She'd been a little afraid of its eerie desolateness. "There's nothing out there."

"I know," Xander agreed. "And there was a red circle drawn around part of it on the map. Weird, huh?"

"That's one way of putting it."

It didn't make sense. The map or the orders for panther blood. She remembered Eugenia's strange acceptance that the Kincaids didn't keep it in stock.

As if she'd expected it all along.

"What about the other two rooms?" Claire asked. "The ones you looked through while I was in Eugenia's?"

Xander shook his head. "Nothing. Other than some clothes in the closet and an iPod in one of them, it almost looked like nobody was even staying there."

She pulled out her phone.

"What are you doing?" Xander asked.

"Looking at the pictures I took of those letters."

She scrolled through the photos, but the screen was too small and enlarging only made everything blurry.

"This is impossible," she sighed. "I'm going to have to upload these to my laptop." She put her phone away and turned to Xander. "Maybe we should bring in the Guild."

He shook his head. "No way. Not yet. Not until I know what my mom was doing with that guy, Maximilian."

"This is serious, Xander. They have pictures of the Guild firstborns." She hesitated. "And I've been thinking . . ."

He turned to her. "What?"

"What if those photographs are tied to the house break-ins?"

He narrowed his eyes. "What do you mean?"

"Think about it. There were Xs drawn through some of the pictures, right?"

"Allegra, the Valcours, Daniel, Laura . . ." he murmured, meeting her eyes. "All the families who've had break-ins."

"Exactly. And if it's true, it means that the photographs that didn't have Xs—"

"Like mine," Xander interrupted.

Claire nodded. "Yours and Sasha's. If I'm right, your houses could be next."

"I guess," Xander agreed. "But we all have antiques, art, electronics. Nothing was taken."

"Exactly."

Xander thought about it. "You think whoever's responsible for the break-ins was looking for something personal?"

"Why else would someone go to the trouble of breaking in to all those houses—houses that are part of the Guild—and not take anything while they were there?"

Claire might not be a believer, but she knew that

personal items were collected to create love spells, protection, or hexes.

And she was pretty sure they could rule out protection and love.

"I don't know . . ." Xander said.

"Do you have a better idea?"

"No," he admitted.

"Which is why we should tell the Guild."

He looked into her eyes. "I thought you didn't believe."

"I don't. But . . . I don't know." Claire turned her head to the window, thinking. "The fact that someone's trying to hurt you—to hurt the Guild—worries me."

"And what if there's more to it than that?" Xander asked. "What if there's something my mom has done that could hurt my dad?"

Claire knew what he was suggesting. The conversation between Estelle Toussaint and Maximilian behind the carriage house had felt oddly personal, even intimate.

Claire reached for Xander's hand. "I'm sorry. I don't know what to say. I'm just worried."

She thought of Sasha. Of her goodness and the accepting way she looked at life that made it easier for Claire to accept things, too.

"It just doesn't seem right to keep quiet," Claire said softly. "What if something happens to you? To them?"

Xander turned his face toward hers. "If you don't believe, you have nothing to worry about."

She sighed. "But if these people do and they're out to hurt someone, they could find another way to do it."

Xander looked ready to argue her point, but a second later his shoulders sagged.

"You're right. I don't want anyone to get hurt, either. I just . . . I need some time to get my head around this. To get a better handle on what my mom has to do with that guy, Maximilian." He stopped talking, and Claire could see the wheels turning in his mind before he started up again. "What if we figured out the letters first? See if there's something in there that will help us?"

"Xander . . ." she started. "Look, I'm as curious about them as you are. I just don't know what some old letters could have to do with your mom and Maximilian."

"Probably nothing, but at the very least, we'll have more information for the Guild when we take everything to them." He paused again. "Please, Claire. It will give me a couple more days to figure out how to tell my dad."

She was torn. Could she live with herself if they waited and something happened to the other firstborns? If something happened to Sasha or Xander?

Could she live with herself if she forced Xander to go public and his family imploded because of it?

"Okay," she finally agreed. "I'll upload them tonight. But at least let me tell Sasha."

Xander shook his head. "I don't want anybody else from the Guild to know yet."

"I get that, but I have a bad feeling about this, and I think we're both too close to it. Besides, we might need help. The letters aren't the only piece of the puzzle. There's that group photograph, too."

"I don't know . . ."

"Sasha's my best friend. I owe it to her to warn her. If I tell her not to say anything, she won't," Claire continued. "Plus, she might know something we don't. Her family's been a member of the Guild almost as long as ours have."

"You sure we can trust her?" Xander asked.

"Positive. We're meeting for yoga tomorrow. I'll tell her then."

He nodded, the worry in his eyes transforming him from the Xander she knew who could handle everything to someone who wasn't sure about anything. He knew his mother wasn't perfect, but he'd always held Estelle on a pedestal. The possibility that she might not deserve his adoration was something he wasn't prepared to deal with.

"Hey." Claire leaned over, touching her lips gently to his. "Everything will be okay. We'll figure this out."

She reached for the door handle, stepping out of the car.

Xander's voice pulled her back. "Claire?"

She ducked down, meeting his brown eyes across the leather seats. "Yeah?"

"Speaking of bad feelings . . . Don't you think it's a little weird that you're the only one of the firstborns whose picture wasn't on that wall?"

Claire swallowed the dread in her throat. "Yeah, but until we know what it means, there's no point stressing about it." She smiled. "Now stop worrying about me. I'm fine. Text me later."

She shut the door before he could say more.

She started walking, knowing Xander would follow her in the car until he knew she was home safely.

His words rang in her ears. Even with Maximilian and Eugenia, Claire was set apart from the other firstborns.

The question was: Did it mean she was safe or that she was in more danger than anyone?

⁓

"Claire? Is that you?"

Claire followed the sound of her mother's voice into the living room. Pilar was sitting in a chair by the window, reading by the light of an old fringed lamp on an end table that had belonged to Claire's grandmother.

"Hey," Claire said. "Where's Dad?"

Her mother waved her hand in the general direction of the rest of the house. "In his study, I think. Was that the Toussaints' car I saw out front just now?"

Claire's pulse stuttered while she scrambled for a reply. "I have no idea. I walked home." She was immediately ashamed of the lie, both because it was told to her mother and because it was a blatant denial of her relationship with Xander.

"Hmmm." Her mother's brow furrowed. She shook her head. "I could have sworn it was theirs, but I must have been mistaken."

"Yeah . . ." Claire stood there silently, wanting suddenly to tell her mother everything.

"Claire?" Her mother was speaking to her. "Are you all right?"

Claire sighed. "I'm just tired. I think I'll go upstairs and rest before dinner."

Her mother was silent, pinning Claire with the icy gray gaze that seemed like it could penetrate all of her most secret thoughts.

"You may as well," she finally said. "That's what summer is for."

She turned back to her book, and Claire headed for the stairs, her feet leaden as she climbed.

TWELVE

Resting was out of the question. Claire's mind was spinning with everything that had happened, her body still amped from the escape she and Xander had made from the house on Dauphine.

She uploaded the photos from her phone to her laptop, scrolling past the group picture and focusing on the letters. She enlarged them until she could make out most of the words, then hit PRINT.

There were three letters, starting with July 31, 1880, and ending with May 25, 1881. She put the French versions aside and turned her attention to the ones Xander had said were translations.

She put them in chronological order and started with the letter marked July 31.

July 31, 1880

Dearest Sorina,

It was with pleasure and surprise that I received your letter. I remember your father well and know he would be pleased that you continue his interest in the craft. I do not know how your country differs from America, but here it seems the new and modern impose at every turn. I've always said that progress is well and good, providing we don't forget the importance of the past.

As for your interest in the darker parts of our art, my answers to your questions must also contain a warning. The craft is a higher calling, though many would vilify it. When used for its intended purpose, it can bring together those destined to love, heal those who are ill, and protect one from rogue spirits and energy.

With that warning, I must assume your questions about black magic are theoretical, and I have never been one to believe in keeping that which we fear in the dark. There, it grows and festers into something dangerous. Better that we should acknowledge all aspects of our craft and teach each generation to respect them in all their diversity.

It is, indeed, possible to curse someone with negative energy, though I advocate only spiritually positive uses of the craft. The recipes for cursing, hexing, and crossing are as old as those used to heal and protect, though passed down less now that reason has gained solid footing for most in the Guild.

As to whether or not I maintain my own crossing spells, it is irrelevant, as I don't make it a practice to use black magic or to pass on that knowledge to my progeny or apprentices. I most humbly ask you to uphold this same standard, as it is one long held among those in our society.

I hope this letter finds you well and that you and your brother are getting along without your parents. I will light candles for you this evening and chant an abundance spell in your name.

> *Warmest regards,*
> *Marie Leveau*

Claire looked up, blinking and trying to bring herself back from another time and place. It sounded like the girl named Sorina had written to Marie for advice about hexing someone.

That anyone would even attempt to get that kind of information from Claire's great-great-grandmother was a surprise. It was well known that Marie the First was a devout Catholic and abhorred black magic of any kind.

Even more puzzling, Marie didn't sound like the superstitious high priestess Claire imagined when she thought about her great-great-grandmother.

Claire stared at the words, trying to get her head around what the letter meant, not only for the situation with Maximilian, but for her own perception of Marie and the craft that defined them both in such different ways.

She finally gave up and lowered her eyes to the second letter.

December 19, 1880

My Dear Sorina,

It is with some distress that I received your last correspondence. I thought the warnings in my previous letter, though mild in the interest of the long-standing friendship between our families, would have deterred you from this path.

I must caution you against further experimentation. Your mother and father would not wish to see you dishonor yourself and the craft in their names. They knew, as we all come to know, that everything has its time. And while their ending may have seemed premature—and certainly it was cruel—they would have said it happened just as God meant for it to happen.

The craft is a force all its own and not to be trifled with. That your desire for revenge has brought you to the brink of the dark arts is testament to your desperation, and it is never wise to travel the paths of the craft with desperation or anger at the forefront of one's mind. It is far too easy for the darkness within to take over completely, enhancing the strength of a spell so that even its creator can no longer control it. That you have come so close to achieving success with this dubious spell brings me such horror I can hardly sleep, though it is true that I have not been well of late in any regard.

It is with these words that I beg you to cease your experimentation. I, of course, will have no part of it. Please consider this my formal refusal of assistance together with a warning. Should you continue along this path, your membership in the Guild—and sadly, that of

*your brother's—will be terminated and we will be unable
to offer you assistance of any kind thereafter.*

*I humbly ask you to honor me, to honor your parents
and all that they stood for, by discontinuing these dark
experiments with the craft.*

They will be your ruin.

Marie Leveau

The words of the letter echoed through Claire's mind
as she finished reading.

Experimentation? What kind of experimentation
was Marie talking about? What was this woman, Sorina,
doing that would have earned Marie's disapproval?
That would have cost Sorina her membership in the
Guild?

And what had happened to Sorina's parents that
would cause her to approach Marie so boldly for a spell
to exact revenge?

Claire shook her head and turned to the final letter.

May 25, 1881

Dear Sorina,

It is with regret that I must inform you of your expulsion from the Guild.

I have listened in horror as accounts of your repeated attempts, and recent success, at using the Cold Blood spell have reached New Orleans. It saddens me greatly that my words of warning fell on deaf ears, for I fear you have used the craft to cross from the world of light into one of such utter darkness that it will surely devour you and any in its path.

It was never my intention that my spells and potions be used for ill. I have uncovered keys to the craft's darkest door only to foil those with a less altruistic view of it, hoping to have some defense should it be used as a means to harm others.

It is a heavy burden to know that my attempts at safeguarding the world from those who would use the craft for evil have instead caused that evil to be unleashed.

I simply cannot suffer it, especially now, as it has become clear that my time in this world is short.

I can only appeal to the all-powerful loas to accept an addendum to the Cold Blood spell. One that will require an ingredient you will never obtain.

It is all I can do, and I can only hope as I prepare to leave this world for the next that you find enough peace in your heart to suspend this wicked game.

Marie Leveau

Claire set the letters down, her great-great-grandmother a palpable presence in the room. Whatever Sorina had done, whatever spell she had conjured, it was enough to scare even Marie.

But there were too many other questions. They twisted and turned through Claire's mind, one running into the next until her head started to hurt, her mind so full of Marie's words that she only wanted to make it stop.

She closed her laptop. She would have Sasha and Xander look at the letters tomorrow. Maybe they would read something into Marie's words that Claire had missed. Something that would connect Marie and the woman named Sorina to Eugenia and Maximilian.

She hoped so, because right now, the only thing they seemed to have in common was fear—Marie's fear of the woman named Sorina and the ominous sense of danger Claire felt around the man named Maximilian.

THIRTEEN

It wasn't easy to keep her mind clear while Cecile took them through the poses the next day. Claire wanted—needed—to find some clarity, some serenity.

But no matter what she did, which mantras she repeated or how many peaceful images she imagined, she kept coming back to the house on Dauphine. To the man meeting with Estelle in secret and the pictures of Xander and Sasha and the unshakable feeling that they were all in danger.

She was relieved when Cecile finally closed the class with the customary bow and in-unison "Namaste." Rolling up her mat, Claire grabbed her bag as Sasha did the same. Then they stepped onto the street, grabbed their bikes, and headed for the Muddy Cup.

"You planning to tell me what's going on?" Sasha finally asked when they were sitting at their table, the sun softened by the tint on the big picture window.

"What do you mean?" Claire laughed nervously. She planned to tell Sasha about the letters, but she was still trying to figure out how much to say and how to say it in a way that wouldn't make her sound crazy.

"I *mean* we've been best friends ever since we dressed up my cat in ritual garb when we were ten and my mother freaked us out by telling us Boots would get her revenge because cats could lay spells." Sasha's expression softened as she glanced at Claire's cup. "Plus, you're drinking Herbal Unwind, and you only drink that when something's wrong."

"I'm just stressed out," Claire protested. "The last thing I need is caffeine."

"Right. But why?" Sasha asked. "I know you. Something's up."

Claire played with her spoon. She was about to start talking when the empty chair next to Sasha scraped against the floor.

When Claire looked up, it was right into Allegra St. Martin's blue eyes.

"Hey," she said.

"Allegra!" Claire hoped she sounded surprised and not rude.

Sasha was less diplomatic. "Wow, have a seat why don't you?" she said sarcastically, taking a drink of her coffee.

Allegra rolled her eyes. "What? I'm supposed to ask for an invitation?"

Claire gave Sasha a brief glare before turning to Allegra with a smile. "We're just surprised to see you, that's all. What's up?"

Allegra leaned in, her glossy black ponytail hanging over one shoulder. "Why don't you tell me?"

The words hung in the air for what seemed like forever before Claire was able to formulate a response. Even then, it wasn't exactly brilliant.

"Uh . . . What do you mean?"

"Seriously?" Allegra tipped her head, looking from Claire to Sasha and back to Claire again. "That's how you're going to play it?"

Claire was relieved when Sasha stepped in. "Why don't you tell us what you're getting at, Allegra? Save us all time."

Allegra leaned back. "You're keeping secrets. I don't know exactly what they are, but I've been seeing them."

"Seeing them?" Claire repeated.

"I get these . . . visions . . . dreams," Allegra explained. "I don't know. Call them what you want. I don't get them all the time, but when I do, they're almost always right."

Sasha's face was guarded. "And you've been getting them lately?"

"Yeah, but I'm only getting pieces. Something about pictures and . . . letters, I think, and maybe a little girl or something. I can't make sense of it."

"A little girl?" Claire could explain the pictures and the letters, but the little girl didn't fit.

Allegra waved her hand. "Whatever. You know how it is; I can't always see the details right away."

Claire didn't know how it was, but she didn't say anything.

"The point is," Allegra continued, "something's going on. I've been feeling a threat for a long time. A threat against the Guild. But I haven't been able to see it clearly. Then the thing with the panther blood happens, and all of a sudden, I see all this other stuff." She looked pointedly at Claire. "Then, I started seeing you."

"Me?" Claire's stomach turned over. This was the second time that someone from the Guild had told her they'd had a dream or vision involving her.

Allegra nodded. "I think it's all tied together, but the parents have locked lips. No one's talking, not even my mother, and you know how unusual *that* is."

Claire considered her options. She could deny everything. Wait for Allegra to leave and fill Sasha in like she'd planned. But Allegra *knew.* Claire didn't know Allegra well, but she was willing to bet that she wasn't the kind of girl who would just give up and walk away. Not when she sensed a threat *and* a secret.

"What makes you think I know anything?" Claire finally asked.

Allegra shrugged. "Call it a hunch. Only my hunches are better than most."

Xander wasn't going to like it. He hadn't even wanted Sasha to know.

Claire sighed. "Okay, but this is just between us. Between us and Xander. No parents and no Guild until we say so. You have to agree or I can't tell you anything."

"Done," Allegra said without hesitation.

Claire looked at Sasha. "Sash?"

"You're kidding, right?" Sasha sounded offended. "If you tell me not to say anything, I won't say anything. You know that."

Claire's nod was slow as she tried to think of a place to begin. Finally, she reached into her bag and pulled out the letters she'd printed from her computer. She pushed them across the table.

Allegra reached for the stack of paper. "What is this?"

"They're letters. Just . . . look at them," Claire said. "I took them with my phone, but I transferred them to my computer and printed them out. I think they're pretty clear now."

Allegra unfolded the papers and shuffled through them.

"Who talks like this?" she asked, setting them down on the table. "It's like reading Shakespeare."

"Look at the dates," Claire instructed.

Allegra sighed and picked up the letters again.

"Eighteen eighty?" She looked up.

"Turn them over and look at the signature lines," Claire said softly.

Sasha grabbed the stack of paper out of Allegra's hands. She shuffled through the pages, turning them over as she went.

Finally, she looked up to meet Claire's eyes. "These are from Marie the First."

Allegra sat up straighter. "What?"

Sasha looked at her. "Marie the First? Marie Leveau?"

Allegra rolled her eyes. "I know who Marie the First is. It's just . . . Let me see those again."

Sasha handed her the pages.

"Is this really her handwriting?" There was awe in Allegra's voice.

"I think so," Claire said.

"Claire . . . Where did you get these?" Sasha asked

It took Claire a minute to find the words, but once she did, she couldn't stop. She began with the fact that Eugenia Comaneci had known her name, something she'd only told the Guild leadership and Xander. Then she told Sasha and Allegra everything else, only leaving out the conversation she and Xander had overheard between Maximilian and Estelle.

Some secrets weren't hers to tell.

By the time she finished recounting their mission to the house on Dauphine, her hands were shaking.

When she was done, the two girls just sat there, staring at her with something like shock.

"My picture was there, too?" Sasha asked, her voice just above a whisper.

Claire nodded. "But yours and Xander's didn't have Xs. We think the ones that are marked are connected to the families that have had break-ins."

"So the pictures that had Xs—including mine—are the ones whose houses have already been broken into?" Allegra asked.

"Well, we don't know for sure," Claire said. "But it kind of makes sense."

"And what, Xander and I will be next?" Sasha asked.

"I don't know," Claire admitted. "But these letters could be a clue."

Sasha picked up the papers and flipped through them again. "Why not just take them to the Guild?"

"We're going to—eventually. It's . . ." She struggled for a way to explain without exposing Estelle. "It's complicated."

"I think it's smart to keep this from them," Allegra announced.

Sasha looked at her in surprise. "You do?"

Allegra made a sound of frustration. "Come on. Do you really think our parents have any idea how to handle a threat? A *real* threat?" She continued without waiting for their answer. "They've only been in charge for what? Twenty years? And in that time nothing remotely interesting has happened. Everyone's played by the rules and they've just . . . sat back, running their little stores in peace."

Sasha frowned. "Not all of the Guild supply houses are small."

"You know what I mean. The Guild has become

another high society clique. Our mothers are more concerned with headpieces for the ball and which charitable board they're on than with overseeing the use of the craft. And our fathers are more concerned about keeping peace with our mothers. The Guild could be working to keep voodoo relevant. The timing's right. People are into all kinds of stuff: homeopathy, eastern religion, meditation, even paganism has made a comeback. But if the Guild has their way, the world of voodoo will stay a secret, just the way they like it."

Claire blinked in surprise. She'd never heard Allegra speak so passionately about anything.

But that didn't mean she was right.

Claire thought about her mother, saw her kneeling in front of the altar, her face smooth and calm. Claire didn't know about anyone else's parents, but her mother still practiced the craft. Still believed. It was hard to imagine that she didn't want others to believe, too.

"Actually," Sasha said, sounding surprised, "I kind of agree with you."

"Right?" Allegra leaned forward, her excitement at finding a sympathetic ear apparent on her face. "Did either of you ask your parents about the panther blood? About what the Guild planned to do about it?"

"I did," Claire said.

"What did they say?" Allegra kept going. "Let me guess; we've got it all under control. Don't worry your pretty little head about it."

"Not exactly," Claire said.

"Did they give you answers?" Allegra asked. "Even after you attended the meeting?"

"No," Claire admitted.

"Right. Because they don't have any. They're going to look the other way and pretend this—whatever it is—isn't happening, because the truth is they don't know what to do about it. They don't *want* to know." She leaned back in her chair, looking at Claire. "I think we should find out what the letters mean before we tell anyone else. Maybe then we'll be able to figure out what's going on."

Claire wondered when "we" had become not only her and Xander and Sasha, but Allegra, too.

"I guess you have a point," Sasha conceded. "But how? I've never heard of this woman named Sorina. And to call the letters vague is the understatement of the century."

"True," Claire admitted. "But they're all we have." She looked at her phone, checking the time. Xander was waiting for her call. Waiting to hear how it had gone with Sasha. "I have to call—" She stopped herself, remembering that she and Sasha weren't alone.

Allegra raised her eyebrows. "Xander?" She rolled her eyes. "Please. I've known about you two forever."

FOURTEEN

"You know you can't tell anyone about this, right?"

Xander was sitting next to Claire at the Muddy Cup. It had taken her fifteen minutes on the phone to convince him that there was no point keeping Allegra out of things. He'd finally agreed to meet them when Claire swore she hadn't said a word about the possible connection between Estelle and Maximilian.

"I'm on your side," Allegra said. "Anything we give the Guild will just disappear into the Cone of Silence."

Sasha laughed.

"Seriously," Allegra continued. "We'd never know what, if anything, they'd done with the information. And the truth is, it probably wouldn't be much. I don't even think most of them are that powerful. Working potions for love and protection is a whole different thing than dealing with black magic and a threat that could involve all of us. I just don't think they're equipped, you know?"

"Okay," Claire said, shuffling through the letters. "The only thing we have to go on is this woman named Sorina and the spell she and Marie were talking about."

"The Cold Blood spell," Sasha said.

Claire looked around nervously before nodding. "Right. I'm thinking we start at home, check out our family resource material for any mention of Sorina or this spell. Between the four of us, we have some serious voodoo history right under our own roofs."

"My mom keeps some really old recipe books locked up in our ritual room," Allegra said. "I'll see if I can get a look at them."

"Just remember, nobody says anything to the Guild until we all agree," Xander said.

"We can meet here tomorrow and compare notes," Claire suggested.

"Sounds like a plan," Sasha said.

They talked for a few more minutes before Allegra and Sasha got up to leave, Allegra talking nonstop as they moved away from the table. They were almost to the door when Sasha glanced back, mouthing the words, "Help me."

Claire laughed, picking up her bag and following Xander outside.

"I'll give you a ride," he said. "We can throw your bike in the back."

"No thanks," she squeezed his hand. "I want to think, clear my head."

"I'm not crazy about the idea of you riding around the city by yourself with everything that's going on."

She smiled. "I'm fine. It's not that far. Besides, it's not like the firstborns are being snatched off the street. With all the break-ins, I'm probably in more danger at home."

"Great. I feel so much better now," he said sarcastically.

"I love you." She stood on tiptoe to kiss him. "But you worry too much." She lifted her leg over the bike, glancing back at him. "I'll text you when I get home."

She started pedaling. A couple of minutes later, she left the busy streets behind and was gliding through the shade of the towering oaks in the residential district. She wasn't the only one taking advantage of summer. In one front yard, two toddlers ran through sprinklers, squealing and giggling while their mother sat on the porch, flipping the pages of a magazine with a glass of iced tea by her side. Claire passed a couple of girls about her age, deep in discussion as they traversed the cracked, uneven sidewalk. Somewhere in the distance, a lawn mower hummed the sound track to every summer she could remember.

She wondered if it would be different in New York or New Hampshire or Connecticut. If kids ran through sprinklers, if teenage girls shared their secrets on long walks, if everyone mowed their lawn. For a minute, she felt a pang of loss so powerful her heart hurt. The truth was, no matter how much she wanted to get away, New Orleans was her home.

She would miss it.

She was thinking about the people at the house on Dauphine, wondering what could bring such an odd group of people halfway around the world to the Guild's doorstep, when she glanced to the left to make sure she was clear for a turn.

That's when she noticed the car behind her.

In this part of town, the Range Rover stood out like a sore thumb. It was black, just like the one Eugenia and the men had gotten out of in front of the house on Dauphine. Claire looked again, trying to make it casual as she tried to get a glimpse at who was driving. It was hopeless. The windows were tinted just enough to make identifying the driver impossible.

She made the turn, watching in her peripheral vision to see if the car followed her. It did, and her heartbeat picked up its pace, beads of sweat jumping out on her forehead as panic hit her system.

She calculated the distance to home. Probably less than a mile.

She was relieved to see a balding man in plaid pants brushing a fresh coat of white paint on the columns fronting his porch. Across the street, a woman was bent over a flower bed, planting a row of azaleas from under the shade of her wide-brimmed hat.

Claire tried to calm herself with the knowledge of their presence. It's not like whoever was in the Rover would do something to her with witnesses around. Would they?

She focused on the road, on the swiftly closing distance between where she was and her house, now only two streets over. When she turned right at the next corner, she dared a glance behind her, hoping the car wouldn't follow.

It did.

She pedaled faster. One more block. One block and another right turn and her driveway would be there.

A blue SUV came into view, slowly backing out of

one of the driveways. Claire contemplated trying to beat it, going around in an effort to lose the Rover. After a moment's indecision, she hit the brakes, stopping as the car reversed all the way into the street. A look back confirmed that the Rover was still there, idling quietly behind her. She saw the shadow of the driver, but she couldn't even tell if it was a man or a woman.

The driver of the SUV—a woman with a boy in the passenger seat next to her—lifted a hand to Claire before heading down the street. At least someone had been witness to her presence there.

She started moving again, picking up speed, pumping the pedals so hard that she was standing on them as she made the final turn onto her street. She didn't even look back to see if the Rover was still there. She focused on her house, half hidden by old trees and the bushes that seemed to grow wild near the iron gate. Then she was coasting up the driveway, steering her bike into the shelter of Spanish moss hanging from the giant elm tree next door.

She wondered if it was her imagination that someone stared at her from behind the darkened windows of the Rover as it drove past, finally disappearing beyond the edge of the property.

Claire took a hot shower, washing off the sweat and dirt of the day and changing into loose boxer shorts and a T-shirt. Her parents were at some kind of charity event, so she had plenty of time to go through the family spell and potion books.

But there was something she wanted to do first.

The old group photo was still nagging at her, and she opened her computer, looking for the pictures she'd uploaded from the house on Dauphine.

Scrolling through the photos, she stopped on the group picture. Everyone was standing on the lawn, all of them wearing a mix of clothes that looked slightly out of date.

Not quite retro, but not exactly current, either.

She zoomed in as much as she dared, not wanting to lose too much clarity on the faces, and hit the PRINT button. When it was done, she pulled the piece of paper out of the tray and hopped onto her bed, sitting cross-legged against the pillows.

The picture was definitely older. The faded colors in the photograph, the hairstyles, even the bags the women carried shrieked 1990s. The people seemed to know each other. Some of the couples had their arms around each other. That was to be expected. But even a couple of the men were clasping each other on the back, their smiles communicating trust and friendship.

And now she saw something she hadn't seen before; a little girl in a wheelchair. She was at the edge of the group, almost omitted from the picture entirely, staring intensely into the lens of the camera. As if she was looking right at Claire.

She heard Allegra, recalling her visions . . . *and maybe a little girl or something.*

Claire brought the picture closer to her face, studying it more closely, willing her mind to make the connection she knew was there. But nothing was clear, and her subconscious was locked tight.

The problem was, she didn't know what she was looking for.

She crumbled the piece of paper, throwing it across the floor. Then, she got up off the bed and headed downstairs.

FIFTEEN

The house was quiet without her parents home, the only sound coming from the ticking of the big clock in the foyer. She made her way past it, hesitating at the door to the store before using her key to open it. Despite the fact that the store was an extension of the house, as familiar to Claire as her own bedroom, she descended the stairs cautiously.

It wasn't the first time she'd been down here at night, but it felt different. She had to force herself to continue, hurrying to the lamp near the counter as soon as her feet hit the floor, fighting the feeling that something was following her into the empty room.

The light helped a little. She stood for a minute, looking around the store, reassuring herself that it was the same as always, that the bolt was down over the private entrance. Once she'd calmed her racing pulse, she turned to the books that lined the shelves behind the counter.

There were three reference manuals on voodoo history. She flipped through them first, looking for any kind of reference to a woman named Sorina. It was a long shot, and she wasn't surprised when she came up empty. Sorina was probably just a regular practitioner who'd been dealt a bad hand and went a little crazy trying to get revenge for the death of her parents.

Claire scanned the shelves. There were a lot of spell and recipe books.

She was going to be here a while.

She pulled the stool over and started with the top shelf. Working her way down, she skipped over the books geared to specific kinds of potions. Whatever the Cold Blood spell was, she had a feeling it wouldn't be in *African Potions and Recipes for Love* and *Authentic Haitian Voodoo for Health and Wellness*.

By the time she got to the bottom shelf, her vision was blurred and her mind echoed with strange words and phrases. She was flipping through a slim volume titled *Traditional Voodoo for Guidance, Insight, and Justice* when a recipe caught her eye.

It wasn't what she expected. Not Cold Blood or anything even close to it, but a potion titled Gaining Wisdom and Insight.

She hesitated as she glanced over the list of ingredients, thinking about the picture, the one she'd crumpled up and thrown across her room. Spells and potions didn't work. She was almost sure of it.

But there was the truth, admitted only in the privacy of her mind.

The *almost*.

Could she be sure? Would she bet the lives of the Guild on her refusal to believe, to try? Would she bet Sasha's life? Xander's?

She read through the recipe again before moving to the front of the store for a red flannel gris-gris bag. Pulling its little drawstring open, she made her way back to the counter. Then she took several glass jars off the shelves and lined them up in front of her.

She scooped some peach tree leaves out of their container. They dropped into the gris-gris bag with a soft rustle. Working her way down the line of jars, she added sage, verbena, and smartweed. She finished by unscrewing the lid on the jar of Solomon's seal root chips, scooping them out with the little metal shovel and adding them to the bag, too.

She finally dared to bend her nose and take a whiff. She was relieved to find the scent almost pleasant. Most of the concoctions mixed for the craft were rank, and she would be sleeping with this one under her pillow.

She knotted the gris-gris bag at the top so the ingredients wouldn't spill out and put the recipe book back on the bookshelf.

She stood there for a minute, contemplating whether to bother with a spell. She could use the gris-gris bag alone. Lots of people did. But her mother and other members of the Guild believed herb and root magic worked together with spellcraft.

Besides, she still had one more book to look through for the Cold Blood spell.

She set the gris-gris bag on the counter and bent down, pulling back the curtain underneath it to reveal a small iron safe.

She vividly remembered the day it had been installed, on the heels of a theft that had cost them one of Marie's two remaining spell books. Claire had been fourteen when her mother had told her the combination.

"What's inside is as much yours as it is ours," Pilar had said. "You never know when you might need it."

In spite of her impatience to go outside and ride her

new bike, Claire had been flattered to learn that the safe had been coded with her birth date. She used it now, turning the knob right, left, and right again.

The safe opened with a quiet pop.

The book was there, just like she remembered.

She removed it with reverence, her previous disdain for it seeming childish. Whether she believed in the craft or not, her great-great-grandmother had owned this book. Had written in it with her own hand.

That had to mean something.

Scooting onto the stool, Claire lowered her eyes to the cover, letting her fingers gently skim the cracked leather surface. It was a soft, mottled shade of green, dips and ridges where there once might have been letters or images.

She opened the book and read the title page, penned by hand.

Recipes, Potions, and Spells
By the High Priestess
Marie Leveau

She decided to look for the Cold Blood spell first and go back through the book for an Insight spell when she was done. That way, she would be sure not to miss anything.

Turning the pages, she kept her eyes on the title of each spell, passing incantations for love and guidance and protection and good health as she searched for anything resembling Cold Blood.

It wasn't there. In fact, just as she'd expected, there wasn't a single spell for black magic.

Sighing, she turned back to the front of the book and started again, this time looking for something that would work in conjunction with the potion in the gris-gris bag.

She found what she was looking for about halfway through the book in a spell titled Request for Knowledge.

She read through it, the words connecting with a memory from her earliest lessons with her mother. Claire would sit on the stool, legs swinging, hands and mind wandering, while her mother tried to force her to pay attention.

Ancient Priestesses of the light,
Bestow knowledge clear, true, and bright
Grant me power and second sight
As I move through darkness of night.

When the words felt almost familiar, Claire pulled three purple candles from behind the counter. She struck a match and lit each one. Then, staring into the flames, she spoke the words of the spell aloud, trying to ignore the voice in her head that told her she was a hypocrite.

She repeated it three times, the words moving through the empty store like a wraith. She'd never noticed the mystical quality of a spell before. On paper it looked trite, but saying it out loud transformed it into a living thing, a force she could feel.

When she was done, she held still, letting the words find their place, like her mother had taught her. Then she blew out the candles, feeling oddly at peace with her decision as she ascended the stairs, gris-gris bag in hand.

The house was still quiet as she locked the door at the top of the stairs. She was glad her parents weren't home yet. Her mother would have been ecstatic that Claire had shown any interest in the craft, let alone actually tried a spell for her own purposes.

Claire didn't want to give her the satisfaction.

When she got to her room, she shut the door and got into bed. Placing the gris-gris bag under her pillow, she turned out the light. She lay in the dark for a long time, trying to quiet her mind and force herself to sleep.

Finally, she began to drift, the scent of verbena and sage reaching up to her as she moved into the landscape of sleep.

SIXTEEN

The house was noisy, conversation and laughter coming from every direction. She moved unseen through the clusters of people, drifting down the stairs and into the front parlor.

People were standing in groups, many with drinks in their hands, talking animatedly as children ran around them. One of them, a dark-haired boy, knocked a picture frame off an end table. A svelte woman in a linen suit smoothly reached out for his arm, her gaze steely. The boy dropped his eyes, picked up the frame, and returned it to its rightful place.

The woman smiled, patting his cheek. "There's a good boy. Now go outside and play, where you won't do any damage."

The boy ran off. Claire, in her dream state, followed

him down the hall, through the dining room, and onto the back terrace.

Claire's eyes were immediately drawn to a woman, standing with a drink in one hand, a loose dress flowing over her slender body. She looked different, with chunky shoes and her hair falling in waves down her back.

But it was definitely Pilar Kincaid.

Claire floated over the lawn, as invisible as ether, as she wound her way through conversations.

A loud clap sounded near the terrace doors, and Claire turned, her gaze resting on her father, holding a fancy black camera.

He smiled at the crowd. "Time for a picture!" he shouted. "Everybody get together over there, at the side of the house."

The crowd began to move, Claire's mother shepherding everyone to the grassy area at the side of the Kincaid property. The hands of the smallest children were grasped by parents or older siblings, the wriggling little bodies sometimes carried against their will.

There was some confusion as everyone moved into place, couples standing together with their children, the single people standing according to height.

Suddenly, there was a prickle of awareness, the sensation of being seen. Claire followed the energy, her eyes resting on a pale, dark-haired man at the edge of the crowd. He seemed to see her, though no one else did.

Claire recognized him immediately as Maximilian Constantin.

He stood in the back row, in front of a little girl in a wheelchair. The girl was pretty, with deeply black hair and sad blue eyes. Her gaze was fixed in the distance. She seemed to be seeing something beyond the scene in front of her.

Claire's dad—young, with a scruffy beard growing at his chin, though all the other men were clean-shaven—came forward, issuing instructions to the group, telling them to squeeze in. Everyone did, though some laughingly protested.

When everyone was finally in place, her dad backed up a few feet. "Everybody smile," he instructed. "Ready. . . . One . . . two . . . three."

The crowd groaned as the flash went off in a blinding burst of light.

Claire turned, spurred forward by some instinct, an

unseen but guiding hand that pulled her back across the lawn, up the stone steps of the terrace, through the dining room doors.

The noise of the party faded into the background until it disappeared completely.

Now it was night. Table lamps were lit around the house, the crowd long gone.

Claire drifted, finding herself in the study that was her father's domain. Her dad was sitting at his desk, his hands busy under the focused light of the desk lamp. She moved closer, wanting a better look.

It was the photograph, the one she'd seen him take on the lawn. He was putting it inside a wooden frame, pressing it into place and locking the clasps at the back of the frame, a penknife at his side.

He turned the picture over, surveying it with studious eyes as he rose from the chair.

Walking across the room, he stopped next to the fireplace. The wall was already cluttered with photographs, but Claire could see that her dad had cleared a spot for the newest addition. He placed it on a hook, leaning back to analyze its placement. After making a few adjustments to make sure it was even, he turned and went back to his desk.

Claire floated out of the study, continuing toward the stairs. The house faded around her as she went, the edges of her dream-vision slowly fading to blackness.

Then she was in the place between wakefulness and sleep, her mind already trying to grasp the significance of what she'd seen.

SEVENTEEN

Claire wasn't even fully awake when she made her way down the stairs, phone in hand.

The early morning sun streamed in through the sheer curtains on the windows, casting golden light across the hardwood floors.

It was quiet. Her parents must have had a late night.

She approached the door to her dad's study, wondering if it would be locked. She couldn't remember a time—ever—when she had entered the room without her dad inside it. But it was open, and she stepped into the room, closing the door behind her.

She took a minute to familiarize herself with the space. A hulking wooden desk stood in front of two big windows. Claire was surprised to see a small love seat in front of the fireplace. She didn't remember it being there, and she wondered if her dad used it to read or nap or if it was just one of her mother's attempts at interior design.

Her eyes settled on the wall of pictures near the fireplace. It was a kind of nook, shadowed by the bump-out of the chimney. There had always been pictures there, but Claire had never paid attention to them. She vaguely recalled them as old and full of people she didn't know or remember.

She crossed the room until she was standing in front of the wall, her eyes sweeping the collection of photographs until she found what she was looking for.

It was there, near the bottom on the left, beneath a picture of some ancestor and above a photograph of her dad with her uncle Philip before he died.

Right where it had been in her dream

Claire lifted the frame off the wall, careful not to knock any of the ones around it to the ground.

The photograph was eerily familiar. She flashed to the moment in the dream, just before the picture had been taken, and then to the younger version of her dad, placing it there and walking away. She lifted her cell phone, scrolling through the pictures she'd taken in Maximilian's room. When she came to the group photo, she stopped, comparing it to the framed one in her other hand.

It was the same.

No, wait. Not exactly the same.

She looked closer. She saw her dad, head bent as he installed the photograph in the frame, a penknife on the desk at his elbow.

And then, when she looked even more closely, she saw the difference in the photographs.

The one from the house on Dauphine showed all the members of the Guild.

The one on her dad's wall, slightly smaller, a sliver of the photograph shaved off the side.

It wasn't difficult to tell what had been removed on the version in her dad's office. It was the man at the edge of the photograph, the pale, dark-eyed one Claire remembered from her dream, and the little girl in the wheelchair.

Claire stood up straighter, the implications of the discovery hitting her like a lead brick.

Maximilian had been part of the Guild. And not just someone who had a key and a license to purchase product. Someone who had been in the circle of power.

Someone who had been one of them.

و

She sat on her bed, looking at the picture on her phone, trying to figure out what to do next. They had a saying in the Guild.

Once a member, always a member.

The only person Claire knew of who had ever left the organization was Crazy Eddie, and he'd been kicked out.

But something had happened with Maximilian, too. She didn't know what it was or what it had to do with the letters in his bag, but it had been serious enough for the Guild to renounce him completely. For her own father to remove him from the Guild's photographic history.

She was getting ready to call Xander when the house phone rang from the hall. A glance at the clock told her it was only 8:00 a.m., early for a phone call on a Sunday. She hurried out of her room, trying to catch it before it woke up her parents.

"Hello, Kincaid residence, Claire speaking."

"Good morning, Claire," a gruff voice said on the other end of the line. "This is Bernard Toussaint. I'd like to speak to your mother or father."

The voice was even, but there was an undercurrent of tension that Claire felt even through the phone line.

"Um . . ." Claire looked up the stairs, wondering if she should wake her parents.

"It's urgent," Bernard added.

"Oh . . . okay. Hold on."

Claire headed toward her parents' room, the phone still in her hand, and knocked softly on the door.

Her dad appeared a few seconds later, shrugging his robe onto his shoulders. "What is it? Is everything okay?"

"Uncle Bernard's on the phone for you," she said, holding out the cordless phone. "He said it's urgent."

He looked surprised, but he took the phone. "Hello? Bernard?"

Claire made no move to leave. Between the discovery of the picture and the early morning phone call, her curiosity was at an all-time high.

"When?" Her dad's face was very still. He sighed, running a tired hand over his face. "Did they take anything?"

He made some more sounds, spoke a few one-word answers into the phone.

"Fine. Yes. We'll be there as soon as we can." He hung up, staring at the phone like he didn't know what it was.

"What's going on?" Claire asked. "Is everything okay?"

Her dad looked over at her. "The Toussaint house was broken into. We need to get over there right away."

"I can come, too, right?" Claire asked, her mind already turning to Xander. This time, she had no desire to be left out of the Guild's business.

"Of course." He headed back into the bedroom. "Be ready in an hour."

"Wait!" Claire called after him.

He turned, meeting her eyes.

"Everyone's fine. Sophie has been taken to her grand-mother's." He hesitated before continuing. "And Xander's okay, too."

Her shoulders sagged with relief as her dad kissed her forehead. He left her standing in the hall, wondering how long her parents had been keeping her secret.

ﾐ

The Toussaints' driveway was already crowded when Claire's dad pulled up. People were milling around the property, including a few men in suits that Claire assumed were part of the much-whispered about private security team Bernard and Estelle quietly paid to keep the Guild's current headquarters—their house—secure.

Claire wasn't surprised at the lack of "real" law en-forcement. Even though voodoo wasn't illegal, Guild business wasn't something they shared with outsiders.

The house was more crowded than the yard. A locksmith was already at work on the front door, adding an intimidating dead bolt and changing the lock on the original knob. She had no doubt the same thing was taking place on all the doors to the house.

"Mr. and Mrs. Kincaid." Betsy rushed toward them as they stepped through the open door. The distress was visible on her face, and she waved them forward, leading them to the library.

Claire heard the murmur of voices before they reached the room. When they got there, everyone only looked up for a second before returning to their conversations, or in Bridget's case, the drink in her hand.

Estelle sat on a damask-covered chair talking to Julia St. Martin, while Bernard whispered quietly to Reynaud. Estelle's expression was calm despite the fact that her face was pale, her hands gripping the sides of the chair.

Betsy hurried forward, bending to say something to her before she retreated.

"I better go check on Estelle," Claire's mother said, patting her daughter on the shoulder.

Claire spotted Xander in his customary spot at the back of the room. Their eyes met, but he didn't move. She knew that it was for her.

"Go ahead," her dad said, tipping his head slightly to Xander. "I need to speak to Bernard."

She took a deep breath and headed toward Xander. His eyes were guarded, his arms folded across his chest in a gesture of self-protection. It was harder than it had ever been not to put her arms around him.

"Hey," she said softly, standing close to him. "You okay?"

He nodded. "They didn't take anything and no one got hurt, so I guess it could have been worse."

"When did it happen?" she asked.

"This morning while we were at church."

"How did you know if nothing was taken?"

"The alarms on the back door were tripped." He hesitated before continuing. "And stuff was moved around in my room like it had been in Allegra's and the others."

Something cold slithered up her back as he said it.

"And you're sure nothing was taken?"

"Nothing we could see."

She had an image of Maximilian touching Xander's things, looking for something personal. Something Xander wouldn't miss.

"So they're really doing it," Claire said softly, horrified all over again. "They're taking stuff from us."

"Not all of us."

She met his eyes. "Right. Everyone but me."

She felt guilty, like it was her fault she hadn't been victimized. Then she remembered the photograph and her discovery.

"I think I found out something about Max—"

"Not yet," Xander said, looking around nervously. "The meeting's about to start."

Bernard stood and cleared his throat. "As you all know, we suffered a residential break-in this morning while we were at church. The details aren't significant except to say it was very like the break-ins some of you in this room experienced. Nothing appears to be missing. In fact, we might not know at all except for a broken window in the study and some things moved around in Alexandre's room."

"I'd like to know what's really going on," Bridget suddenly demanded.

Even from the back of the room, Claire could see Bridget's hands trembling.

Bernard leveled his gaze at her. "I assure you that we are using every means available to get to the bottom of it. You know as much as we know."

Bridget laughed a little, but it was as brittle as the ice in her glass. "I highly doubt that. I know I'm the newest member here, but that doesn't give you a right to keep me in the dark. Someone broke into my house, too, you know."

"I think we all know what's going on here," Julia St. Martin said quietly.

The room grew hushed as everyone looked at Bernard.

This is it, Claire thought. *He's going to tell the truth. He's going to tell them Max is behind the orders of panther blood, the break-ins, all of it. He's going to explain why.*

"Julia." Bernard's voice was a warning, a low rumble of thunder just before a violent storm. "That will be all."

She sat up straighter, indecision warring across her elegant features. Claire had a flash of Allegra. Saw her strength in the set of her mother's jaw, her stubbornness in the fire lighting Julia's eyes.

"We have to do something," Julia said softly, fear threading her voice.

Claire watched Bernard's face carefully, wondering if it was her imagination that his right eye was twitching a little.

"It's all under control," he said. "My alarm system is

being upgraded as we speak, and I've asked Palmwood Security to consult with each and every one of you before you leave. The Guild will fund immediate upgrades to your stores and residences as you see fit, and we will retain on-site security for those of you who want it until the threat passes."

"And what if it doesn't?" Julia asked.

"It will," Bernard insisted. His eyes dared anyone to disagree.

The room was uncomfortably silent, some of the women fidgeting with their clothes while the men stood quietly by, making it clear they didn't intend to challenge Bernard's authority.

Catching Claire's eye, Xander tipped his head toward the hall. They slipped out the door at the back of the room and headed outside.

EIGHTEEN

Xander took her hand and they followed the path to the arbor, the security men talking and calling out to one another as they worked around the property.

"They're resetting the alarms," Xander explained. "Making them more sensitive, connecting them to every room in the house instead of just the main entrances, and attaching the alarm to my dad's cell so it'll alert him, even when we're out, if someone tries to break in again."

They reached the arbor and Claire dropped onto one of the garden chairs.

. . . we might not know at all except for a broken window in the study and some things moved around in Alexandre's room.

Maximilian had something of Xander's.

And Max was going to use it to hurt him, Claire just knew it.

She tried to focus on what she'd learned, hoping for a

way forward. A way to stop whatever was happening.

"I figured something out," she finally said. "About Maximilian."

Xander sat next to her. "What is it?"

"I couldn't decide why that group picture looked so familiar, but then I . . ." She stumbled, not ready to admit she'd used the craft. There was no proof the gris-gris bag and spell is what had done it. It was only a dream. "I remembered."

"Remembered what?" Xander's brown eyes were full of concern.

"My dad has the same picture in his study, but the one on his wall has a piece shaved off the side. Look." She pulled out her phone, flipping through her pictures, trying not to feel sick when she saw the one of Xander, the one that probably, at this very minute, had an X drawn through it. She stopped when she came to the group photo she'd recorded from the house on Dauphine.

She turned it so Xander could see the screen and pointed to the right edge of the photo, the place where Maximilian stood, his eyes glaring defiantly at the camera, the little girl in her wheelchair in front of him.

"See this man?"

Xander nodded.

"I think it's Maximilian. I mean, he's obviously younger in this photo, but I think it's him."

Xander peered more closely at the image. "Is that . . . my parents? And . . ." He pointed to the woman in the flowy dress. "Your mother?"

Claire nodded. "This is obviously a photo of all the Guild families. More specifically, it's a photo of the families who hold all the power. If you look closely, you can see Allegra's parents and Sasha's and the Valcours. Bridget was pregnant, so it must have been about thirteen years ago, just before Daniel was born." Claire met his eyes. "Maximilian was one of them, Xander. One of us."

Xander's forehead was furrowed as he thought about what she said. "You said part of the picture in your dad's study was cut off?"

"Yeah, this part." Claire pointed to the side where Maximilian stood. "It's like they wanted to pretend he'd never existed. Like he'd never been one of them."

"No one leaves the Guild," Xander said. He shrugged, remembering. "Not willingly."

"Right, which is why my bet is on Maximilian getting kicked out. The question is what happened that would make him target us? And why did he get kicked out in the first place?"

"I don't know," Xander said, pacing. "I don't get any of it."

"Don't get any of what?"

Claire turned toward the voice as Sasha stepped into the arbor.

"Hey," Claire said. "I think I figured something out. I was filling Xander in. Is Allegra coming?"

"Oh, she's coming," Sasha said.

"What's that supposed to mean?" Claire asked.

"It means, that girl could make texting an Olympic sport. I think the longest I went without a text from her last night was three hours, and that was between three a.m. and six a.m. I'm exhausted."

Claire laughed as Allegra entered the arbor, her tan legs a mile long in white shorts. She wore her hair down even though it was nearly a hundred degrees outside. Claire would have been surprised if she'd ever sweat a drop.

"What's so funny?" she asked, sitting down. "What did I miss?"

Sasha rolled her eyes. "Nothing."

Allegra looked suspicious, but a second later she

leaned across the table, her eyes on Xander. "Everyone okay?"

He nodded. "Same MO as the other break-ins. Nothing taken that we could see, but a few things seemed to be moved around in my room."

Sasha looked stricken. "Which means I'm next."

"Unless we can figure everything out first," Allegra said. "And I don't know about you guys, but there's nothing even close to a Cold Blood spell in any of our books. Not even the ones my mom keeps locked up."

"We don't have it, either," Claire said.

"Same," Sasha said. "I looked twice, just to be sure."

"I struck out, too," Xander said. "But Claire found out something about the group picture from the house on Dauphine."

Claire filled them in, explaining how she'd taken a picture of it with her phone.

"It looked familiar to me for some reason," she continued. "It was driving me crazy, so I . . ." She hesitated, wondering why it was so hard to admit that she'd used the craft even if she wasn't entirely sure that's what had caused her to have the dream. "I used an insight potion and a knowledge spell from Marie's book to try and figure it out."

Allegra sat back in her chair. "An insight potion? With the sage and verbena and Solomon's seal chips?"

She nodded, sensing Xander straighten beside her. He would definitely have questions later. She just hoped it could wait until they had everything else figured out.

"Did it work?" Sasha asked.

"I don't know. But something did. I dreamed about the Guild. I saw everybody at some party when we were all little. That guy named Maximilian was there, too. When I woke up, I remembered that my dad had the same picture hanging on the wall in his study. Except when I found it, it was missing the piece with Max in it. I compared it against the one from the house and everything."

"What do you mean it was missing a piece?" Sasha asked.

"Someone—my dad, I think—cut him out of the picture."

Everyone fell quiet, each absorbed in their own thoughts.

"It's weird, right?" Xander finally said. "That Maximilian was part of the Guild?"

Sasha nodded. "Either he did something really, really bad to get kicked out, or the Guild did something really, really bad to him to make him leave."

"Exactly," Claire agreed. "But what?"

"We could ask our parents," Sasha suggested. "If we tell them we know Maximilian used to be part of the Guild, they'll have to give us some kind of explanation."

Claire wasn't so sure. She thought about the aura of secrecy she'd never questioned. About all the things she didn't know about the Guild. True, until now, she'd never wanted to know. But all of a sudden, it bothered her.

"Come on. We all know the Guild isn't talking," Allegra said. "Maybe they'd give us some kind of lame explanation for Maximilian's defection, but it probably wouldn't be the truth. And then they'd know that we've been snooping around. After that, you can say goodbye to us figuring out anything on our own. They'd be watching us like hawks."

"Which is why we have to find out what happened on our own," Claire said. "Wait until we have all the information to confront the Guild."

And until we know what's going on between Estelle and Maximilian, she thought, glancing at Xander.

"How are we going to find out what happened if

nobody's talking?" Sasha asked. "I doubt you're getting into the house on Dauphine again."

Claire took a deep breath. "I think we should talk to Eddie."

"*Crazy* Eddie?" Sasha said too loudly.

"Shhhhh! God!" Claire looked around, hoping no one had overheard.

Xander stopped pacing. "What does Crazy Eddie have to do with anything?"

"Probably nothing," Claire admitted. "But if we want to find out what happened with Maximilian, we need someone who knows a lot about the Guild but isn't loyal to it. I can't think of anybody but Crazy Eddie. Can you?"

Xander dropped into the chair next to her. "I don't know, Claire . . . I thought you wanted to take everything to the Guild?"

"That was before I found out our parents aren't exactly coming clean. They know way more than they're letting on—about the panther blood, the break-ins, and Maximilian. After the orders came in, they held their so-called emergency meeting, but Allegra's right; they never said anything about what they were going to do about it or what was really happening." Claire stood up, walking angrily to the edge of the arbor before she turned back to look at the others. She thought of Xander's mother, talking to Max in secret, like whatever he was threatening could be negotiated. Like it didn't call for an actual response from the Guild. Even if Estelle had been having an affair with Max, her priorities were obviously out of whack.

"If we're right, *we're* the ones in danger. Or . . . you and the others are. They force us to memorize spells and invite us to meetings when we turn eighteen, but now, when something important happens, no one tells us anything. And you know what? I might be able to live with that if I thought they were *doing* something about the threat. But it's not really looking that way, is it? They're not even talking to each other about it."

"She's right," Allegra said.

"I'm not disagreeing," Xander said. "I just don't know what good it will do to talk to Crazy Eddie."

"If we can find out what Maximilian did or what happened that made him leave the Guild," Claire said, "we might be able to figure out his motive. And if we figure that out, we might get an idea of what he's up to and whether or not we're really in danger."

"It's not a bad idea," Allegra agreed. "Plus, maybe Crazy Eddie knows something about Cold Blood."

Sasha shook her head. "You guys are forgetting something: Crazy Eddie hasn't been around for years. No one even knows where he lives."

Claire hesitated, trying to get up the courage to say what she'd been thinking.

"Your dad's the head of membership, Sash," she finally said.

It took a minute for Sasha to get it. "You want me to look in my dad's records?"

"I don't know what else to do," Claire admitted. "We don't even have Eddie's last name."

Sasha shook her head. "First of all, my dad wouldn't let me within five feet of those records. Second, they're all stored inside the computer in his office. And third, no one's heard from Eddie in ages. My dad probably doesn't even have a current address for him."

"What if he didn't know you were looking at the records?" Allegra asked.

"You mean, what if I violate his privacy to find a crazy voodoo guy who was kicked out of the Guild years ago and hasn't been heard from since?" Sasha's eyes were bright, her voice a little too loud.

"Look, it's their fault we have to sneak around. If they'd just come clean, we wouldn't have to do all this.

And if Max is as dangerous as he seems, we're the ones in trouble. *You're* in trouble, Sasha. You and Xander and Laura and everyone else. Do you really trust the Guild to figure it all out before someone gets hurt? The Toussaints' house was broken into *this morning*, so whatever they're doing doesn't seem to be working."

Sasha glared at her. After what seemed like forever, she exhaled loudly. "I see your point. But this is . . . This is big, what you're asking me to do."

"I know," Claire admitted. "I'm sorry. I can't think of any other way."

Sasha stared out the window for a minute before turning back to them. "I'll do it. But I can't do it alone."

Xander turned his palms to the ceiling. "What can we do to help?"

"Not we," Sasha said. "Claire."

Claire looked up in surprise. "Me?"

"My dad works from home. He's home *all the time*. Trust me, I have to listen to my mom yelling at him to get out from under her feet all day long in the summer. Assuming you want Eddie's address sooner than next week, one of us will have to keep him busy while the other one looks on his computer."

"One of us?" Claire asked.

"Probably you," Sasha said. "Because it would be weird for me to leave you alone with my dad while I dig through his office. He'd hunt me down after two minutes to rescue him from having to make conversation."

"What about Xander and Allegra?" Claire asked.

Sasha looked from one to the other of them. "Have I ever invited either of you over to hang out at my house?"

Xander shook his head.

"Point taken," Claire said. "So what do we do?"

NINETEEN

Sasha's house was quiet except for the distant sound of her younger brother, Maddox, playing Xbox in the den.

If Sasha was right, hanging out in the kitchen was their best bet for cornering her dad long enough for Claire to look on his computer. Sasha's dad drank coffee all day, every day. It was only a matter of time before he emerged from his study to top off his cup. Her mother was doing the grocery shopping and wasn't home.

"Want some sweet tea or something?" Sasha asked her.

Claire nodded nervously. "Sure."

Sasha poured the tea and they sat at the kitchen island, waiting.

Claire took a drink from her glass. "So tell me again what I'm looking for."

"I honestly don't know," Sasha said. "I don't dig around

in my dad's work. I'd say go to all the document folders first. Look for a main folder that has to do with the Guild and then a sub folder titled Addresses or Contacts or Members or something."

"And we don't have a last name for Crazy Eddie?" Claire asked.

"I've been trying to remember it. I know I've heard it before, but it must have been a long time ago. Just look for any name with Ed, Eddie, or Edward. We can compare them against existing members later if we have to."

Claire nodded, rubbing her sweaty palms on the side of her shorts. "What if you can't keep him in here long enough?"

She patted something on the counter. "Taken care of."

"What's that?" Claire asked.

She held it up. "The Louisiana State DMV rule book. I finally convinced him I'm ready to take my road test. I'll ask him to quiz me."

"What if he says he's busy or he has to get back to work or something?"

Sasha thought about it. "I'll say something really loud. Something like . . . 'Do you want me to make you a sandwich, Dad?'"

Claire laughed. "A sandwich?"

"Yeah, I could kind of shout it when he turns to leave without it seeming too weird. If you've got something better, I'm listening."

"I don't," Claire admitted. "But won't he be suspicious?"

"I don't think so. I make him lunch sometimes when I make my own, especially when my mom's not home. It's the most normal thing I can think of."

"All right," Claire agreed. "I'll listen for the sandwich."

They turned as they heard someone making their way down the hall, the footsteps purposeful and heavy.

"Sasha? You home?" her dad called. He stepped into the kitchen. "Well, hello, Claire. I didn't know you were here."

"Hi, Mr. Drummond. How are you?"

"I'm fine, thank you. And you? How are your parents?"

Moving through the expected niceties of conversation was second nature. She was pretty sure her first word wasn't "mommy" or "daddy" but "please" or "thank you." It had been bred in Claire since she could speak.

"We're all fine. Thank you for asking."

He moved to the coffeepot on the counter, preparing to fill his cup.

This is it, Claire thought, her stomach in knots. *Do it now. Do it for Xander and Sasha.*

"Excuse me," Claire said. "I'll be right back."

She was counting on the fact that Sasha's dad would assume she was going to the restroom and wouldn't say anything. He didn't.

Claire tried to be leisurely as she left the kitchen, but once she was in the hall, she booked it to Mr. Drummond's study.

She was careful not to bump the door, already half open, on her way in. It was easy to feel someone else's presence, to notice little things that had been moved or were out of place, when you were intimately familiar with a room.

She took a few seconds to orient herself. She couldn't remember a time when she'd been in Mr. Drummond's study, and she took in the large, ornate rug in the center of the room, the Haitian and African art on the walls. The desk dominated one area of the room, a sleek laptop open on its surface.

She forced her feet to move, her heart thudding in her

chest every step of the way, adrenaline surging through her veins at the possibility of being caught.

Moving around to the other side of the desk, she let her hand graze the touchpad. The black screen lit up, opening to a spreadsheet that seemed to contain expense reports or something. She minimized it, feeling guilty for even glimpsing the Drummonds' private finances.

Luckily, Mr. Drummond used a Mac. It made everything a little bit easier, and she started by pulling up the Finder. She chose Documents first, relieved when a folder labeled GUILD appeared. She clicked on it, sucking in her breath when it opened to reveal multiple subfolders and more documents than she could count. How much paperwork did it take to be head of membership for such a selective organization?

The answer, apparently, was a lot.

Labeled by country, there were folders for England, Ireland, Scotland, France, Spain, Germany, and almost every European country she could think of, including countries in Eastern Europe. Her eyes lingered on the folder labeled GUILD_ROMANIA, but she continued down the list.

She didn't have time to browse.

She glanced at the door of the study, listening for

sounds from the hallway, before clicking on the folder titled GUILD_NOLAHQ.

It didn't exactly narrow the field. There were dozens of documents.

She started at the top, scrolling down and trying to gauge the contents of each file from its title. She had no idea how long she'd been gone. But it was only a matter of time before Sasha ran out of ways to keep her dad in the kitchen.

The amount of paperwork was dizzying. There were reports for dues and other membership expenses, documents that seemed to have something to do with narrowing the qualifications for membership in the Guild, and finally, something labeled CONTACT_INFO.

She clicked on it, and it opened to reveal a spreadsheet with names, addresses, and phone numbers.

Jackpot.

It was alphabetical by last name. She started at the top, skimming the list for someone that could be Crazy Eddie. She came across six Edwards, but they were all families whose last name she recognized. She started again, looking more closely.

And this time, she found what she was looking for.

Edward "Eddie" Clement.

Next to his name was an asterisk. She looked at the bottom of the document for a key. There it was: another asterisk with the word "INACTIVE" next to it.

She continued scrolling, wanting to make sure there weren't any others. But no. Eddie Clement was the one and only name with the asterisk that denoted inactive membership.

Voices rose from the kitchen. Claire's eyes darted to the door, and she held stock-still for a few seconds, listening for Sasha's code words. They didn't come.

Pulling her phone out of her pocket, she made a note of Eddie's address.

"Do you want me to make you a sandwich before you go back to work, Dad?"

Sasha's voice carried through the house.

"Damn," Claire muttered, eliminating the screen with the addresses, backtracking through every document until the screen was empty. She half expected Mr. Drummond to appear in the doorway of the study while she brought his original document back up.

When everything on the screen looked the way it had when she got there, she slid out from behind the desk and started for the door. She was almost out of the room when she remembered something.

The screensaver had been up when she'd first gotten into the study.

Sasha's dad called out, his voice too close to the study for comfort. "Ham and cheese, but would you mind bringing it to me? I have to get back to work."

Claire ran back to the computer and hit the keys that would put the computer in sleep mode. She was at the study doors when she heard Mr. Drummond's footsteps coming to the bend in the hall.

She slipped out of the study, trying to slow her breathing down. She came to the powder room just as Mr. Drummond's feet appeared at the end of the hallway.

Ducking into the half bath, she closed the door and turned on the light. Waiting, she listened as he approached. Then she opened the door and turned off the light, trying to act surprised to run into him in the hallway.

"Oh! Hey, Mr. Drummond."

"Hello again, Claire. Nice to see you. Tell your parents hello."

"Will do."

They went their separate ways, Mr. Drummond toward his study and Claire toward the kitchen, where

Sasha was waiting. When she got there, Sasha looked at her with terrified eyes.

"Did you get caught?"

Claire collapsed onto the tile floor, lying on her back. "No."

"And?"

Claire lifted her head, pulling out her phone and holding it up. "I think I got it."

TWENTY

By the time Claire texted Xander to let him know she had an address for Crazy Eddie, it was too late for them to go looking for him. The Treme District was iffy during the day.

She wasn't about to go there after dark.

They agreed to go the next morning. They would meet up afterward with Sasha and Allegra at the Cup.

Claire tossed and turned all night. Her dreams were full of things she didn't understand. Fires and chanting and powder being blown in her face while drums beat out a rhythm that seemed to move through her bones, the scent of sage and verbena drifting to her on the winds of her dreams.

The smell woke her up, heart racing. Sweat slicked her forehead and dampened the hair at the back of her neck. She reached under her pillow, pulling out the gris-

gris bag. Was it possible that it was the source of her dreams? That the craft her parents and the Guild believed in was real and trying to show her something she didn't yet understand?

Lying back down on her pillow, she threw the gris-gris bag across her room.

She didn't dream again.

Xander picked her up at ten and they headed toward Treme. They had just gotten on North Rampart when Xander reached over Claire's knees, opening the glove box with one hand while he drove with the other.

"What are you doing?" Claire asked.

He shut the compartment and handed her something. "Giving you this."

She took it reflexively, opening her palm to a tiny gris-gris bag on a leather cord.

"What is it?"

He took a deep breath, like he was bracing himself for something difficult. "It's a potion I worked for protection." She started to protest and he stopped her. "Just listen to me for a minute, okay?"

She hesitated before nodding. "Okay."

"I'm still having dreams, Claire. And they're all about you. I see you tied up and bleeding, just like I did that first day. I can't see his face, but the Houngan is chanting, working a spell to use your blood." He glanced at her, his face turning dark before he looked back at the road. "I can't get to you, Claire. I don't know why. But I feel far away, and the place where you are, it's . . ." He shook his head. "I don't know. It's hard to reach or something. I . . ." He swallowed hard, glancing at her again. "Just wear it, okay? For me?"

She looked down at it, catching a whiff of aloeswood. It was a small thing, wearing the gris-gris for Xander. And maybe it wasn't just for him. For the first time, she had a legitimate reason to question her disbelief.

She put the cord around her neck. "I'll wear it. Thank you."

His face relaxed before her eyes, and she realized what it cost him, worrying about her. She reached for his hand, lifting it to her lips.

"What are we going to do if this isn't Crazy Eddie's address?" Xander asked, changing the subject.

"I don't know," Claire said. "We have to hope that someone would know where he went. My mom once told me that in New Orleans, most people spend their whole lives in the same neighborhood. I guess we have to hope she's right."

Xander grew quiet, and Claire turned her face to the window. Treme was a completely different world from her little corner of the city. Fascinated by the Creole architecture and the African flags flying from crumbling porches, she suddenly felt embarrassed. She'd lived in New Orleans her whole life and had never once been to this part of town.

She was thinking about that—about the fact that people and things and places could be right under your nose and you might not know them at all—when a black SUV pulled up next to the Mercedes. The panic was instinctual. She didn't even have time to feel it build, to talk herself down. It didn't matter that the SUV wasn't a Range Rover. All she could see was the car that had followed her home from the Cup, the slow drive-by it had done when she'd finally reached the safety of her driveway.

A minute later, the SUV accelerated, passing them and turning right at the next corner. Claire took a slow, deep breath. *Get it together. You're losing it.*

"You okay?"

She looked up, following Xander's eyes to her fingers, nervously tapping the armrest of the door. She didn't want to tell him about the man who'd followed her from

Lafayette back to Myrtle's, about the Rover that had seemed to be following her home. He'd only worry. He might even tell her parents, and there was no way to do that without telling them everything else.

"A little nervous," she admitted.

"I can't say that I blame you."

The voice on the GPS announced that they'd arrived at their destination, and Xander pulled next to the curb. He glanced out the windows, looking for numbers on the houses as she did the same. If they were there, Claire couldn't see them.

The street was lined with small stucco structures, the windows all barred. Many of the houses still had circles and numbers spray painted on the outside from the recovery efforts after Hurricane Katrina, and Dumpsters still lined the streets in greater number than the cars parked there.

The area bore almost no resemblance to the leafy, shady New Orleans that Claire called home. This was a distant relative, stark and hard with no relief from the sun that beat down on the concrete that surrounded them.

"You ready for this?" Xander asked softly.

"Yeah."

They got out of the car, and he locked the doors with the remote. When they stepped onto the curb, he walked up to a guy sitting there with a trash bag full of stuff.

"Hey, want to make a quick forty dollars?"

The guy blinked a couple of times, like he couldn't believe his luck. "Forty dollars?"

"Yeah," Xander said. "All you have to do is watch that car. Make sure nobody messes with it." He took a twenty-dollar bill out of his wallet and handed it to the guy. "I'll give you the other twenty when I come back."

The man's eyes were full of suspicion, but he took the money, stuffing it into his pocket.

"You know where Eddie Clement lives?" Xander asked him.

The man shook his head without even thinking about the question.

"Okay, thanks, anyway. We'll be right back."

They turned their attention to the house in front of them. Claire scanned the street, wondering if maybe they'd missed the house numbers from the car, but it was just like she thought; none of the houses had any identifying characteristics.

"Now what?" she asked.

Xander pointed to some guys huddled on the porch of a house a couple doors down. "I guess we'll have to ask them."

Claire swallowed her nervousness. "Right."

She could hear the men laughing and talking as they approached. When they spotted Claire and Xander, a murmur went up through the group. They were all quiet by the time Xander started up the walk, his hand firmly on Claire's arm.

"Hey," Xander said. "How's it going?"

Claire was surprised by the change in Xander's voice, in his mannerisms. He was still Xander. Still dressed in nice clothes with the manners of an old-school Victorian. But now his speech was slightly slower, the words almost running together, and instead of standing perfectly straight, he was slouched just a little.

She didn't know if the change was because of the neighborhood or the fact that they were around a bunch of guys. Maybe a little of both.

One of the men, tall with a chest the size of a wine barrel, stepped forward a little. "Good, good. What can we do for you, my brother?"

"I'm looking for Eddie Clement. Any idea where he lives?"

"Eddie Clement?" the man said. "Crazy Eddie Clement?"

The men erupted into peals of laughter, muttering to one another words that Claire couldn't quite make out.

"That would be the guy," Xander confirmed. "Crazy Eddie."

Their laughter slowly subsided. The man in front slid his gaze to Claire before turning his eyes back to Xander. "Shit, man. Crazy Eddie moved after Katrina."

Claire's heart sunk a little.

"Any idea where he went?" Xander asked.

"Don't no one 'round here go far," the man in front said. "Crazy Eddie moved three blocks north. Used to live there." He pointed to a house across the street, its roof caved in, a dark, moldy waterline just under the eaves.

Xander nodded in understanding.

It was easy to forget there were places in New Orleans, not far from where Claire lived, that were still totally devastated by Hurricane Katrina. She'd always thought of herself as a strong person, but these people were stronger than her by a mile.

"Any idea which house?" Xander asked.

"For Eddie?" the guy on the porch confirmed.

"Yeah."

The guy thought about it and then turned to confer with the group behind and around him. They spoke softly to one another for a couple of minutes before the guy in front turned back to face Xander and Claire.

He pointed to a street on the left. "Take that three blocks up. It's the green house on the corner. Probably see Miss Thelma on the porch."

Xander stepped forward, extending his hand. "Thanks."

The man looked at his hand in surprise before stepping forward slowly. He clasped Xander's hand in his own.

"No problem, man." His eyes drifted again to Claire. "Watch your girl up there, now."

Xander nodded, his jaw tight. "Always."

He steered Claire down the walk. Claire could feel the eyes of the men on the porch as she and Xander headed for the street on the left. She breathed a sigh of relief when they turned the corner, though it wasn't any better here.

"You okay?" Xander asked softly. "I could take you home. Come back alone."

"No way," Claire said. "I'm fine."

They continued up the street. Most of the houses

looked like the ones where they'd parked; water-damaged, condemned stickers on the front, and roofs caved in with only a few semihabitable structures still standing.

The Guild didn't discriminate according to wealth. You got in because of your heritage, your connection to the old voodoo families that helped establish the city. Still, because of the niche market, most of the supply houses did well—somewhere between middle class and really affluent like the Toussaints, who catered to the oldest, richest families and to authentic wholesalers.

This didn't look like a place for a Guild member, and Claire couldn't help wondering if Crazy Eddie regretted whatever he'd done to get kicked out.

"Think that's it?" Xander was pointing to a house on the corner up ahead. The siding was only slightly green, faded now from water and sun.

"I don't know. Maybe."

A figure became visible on the porch. As they came closer, Claire saw that it was an old woman, swaying back and forth in an old-fashioned rocker and staring off into the distance.

"That must be Miss Thelma."

Xander nodded, loosening his hold on her arm a little when he realized no one was around but an old lady in a housecoat.

They approached the porch slowly, not wanting to startle the old woman. Even when they stopped at the bottom of the stairs, her only acknowledgment of their presence was the movement of her eyes in their direction. She didn't pause in the rhythm of her rocking.

Xander seemed to hesitate.

Claire cleared her throat before speaking. "Hello. You must be Miss Thelma."

Silence stretched between them. Claire was preparing to repeat herself when the old woman spoke.

"Maybe, maybe not. Who's asking?" Her voice was cracked and low with an undercurrent of sharpness. Old woman or not, Claire wouldn't want to mess with her.

Claire stepped forward and held out a hand. "I'm Claire Kincaid. This is my friend Xander Toussaint. We're actually looking for Cr—" Claire stumbled over the nickname, realizing it probably wasn't polite—or smart—to put the word "crazy" in front of someone's name when you didn't know exactly who you were talking to.

"Eddie," Claire finished. "We're looking for Eddie Clement. We were told he might live here."

"Might be, might not." The woman was still rocking.

"We're not looking to give him any trouble," Xander said. "We were just hoping he could help us."

"What folks like you be needing help from Eddie for?" she asked, her eyes shrewd.

Claire swallowed hard, debating their options. On the one hand, she hated to give too much away to someone she didn't know. Even an old woman like this could be connected to the Guild one way or another.

On the other hand, Crazy Eddie was their only hope for information about Maximilian without going directly to the Guild.

"We were kind of hoping Eddie might be able to answer some questions," Claire said. "About the Guild."

It was a test. A risky one, but necessary. Either the woman would know what she was talking about or she wouldn't, but at least they'd know who they were dealing with.

For a split second, the woman paused in her rocking. She started up again, but it was enough for Claire to know she'd gotten the woman's attention.

"What Guild you say?" The woman's question was sly, but Claire wasn't playing.

Miss Thelma knew exactly what Guild, and Claire looked at her without flinching until she spoke again.

"He's inside." She tipped her head to the door. "You go on in, but don't be giving my Eddie any trouble now, ya hear?"

Claire nodded, stepping onto the porch. "Thank you."

Xander followed her up the steps, stopping when Miss Thelma reached out, lightning fast, and grabbed his arm.

She tipped her head at Claire. "You best be watching her now."

Xander nodded. "Yes, ma'am."

Claire reached for the screen and glanced back at Miss Thelma, wondering if they were supposed to knock or ask permission. But the old woman was back to her rocking, and Claire pulled open the door. The squeaky springs would announce their presence to whoever was inside anyway.

They stepped into a hallway, the light minimal, barely leaking from the rooms on either side. Hesitating, Claire listened for something that would tell them where Crazy Eddie might be. A television, a radio, anything.

But it was deathly still.

Xander stepped in front of her. She recognized it as

one of his many protective maneuvers. Letting Claire take the lead with an old woman was one thing. Letting her lead the way through a house in Treme when they had no idea who was inside?

There was no way Xander would let that fly.

He reached back for her hand. They passed a narrow, decrepit staircase and looked into the first two rooms to the left of the hallway. They were tiny, one a living room and the other a bedroom. Both were empty.

Continuing down the hall, they passed what looked like a closet and headed for the back of the house. Light streamed from the room at the end of the hallway. They headed toward it, Claire sending a silent prayer to whoever was listening for Crazy Eddie to be there. She was definitely not up for exploring the second level. Her heart was already beating too fast.

They reached the door to the back room. Xander hesitated, looking back at her before shrugging and pulling her into the room with him.

A man sat at an old Formica table, a book in his hand and a glass of what looked to be sweet tea at his elbow. He was so engrossed in what he was reading that he didn't seem to notice them enter the room.

Xander cleared his throat. "Excuse me." The man didn't

move a muscle or give any indication that he was startled. Xander continued. "Are you Eddie Clement?"

The man didn't look up. Just held up a finger, gesturing for them to wait, as he continued reading. They stood in silence as he read, finally turning the page and bending the corner to save his place.

He closed the book and looked up at them. "You're here about the Guild."

TWENTY-ONE

Claire watched Eddie move around the tiny but immaculate kitchen as he poured them sweet tea.

He wasn't anything like what she'd expected.

For one thing, he didn't look crazy. In fact, he looked decidedly *uncrazy*, his eyes clear behind glasses with round black frames. His jeans were immaculate, topped with a loose tunic-type shirt adorned with an African print. Before he'd gotten up to get the tea, Claire caught a glimpse of the book he was reading; *Moby-Dick*.

Not exactly light reading.

"How did you know we were from the Guild?" Xander asked.

"I've been seeing you," Eddie said, his back to them as he poured.

"Seeing us?" Xander repeated.

Eddie brought the glasses to the table and set them in front of Claire and Xander.

He tapped the side of his head. "Up here. Mostly when I sleep." He sat down, the chair's chrome legs squeaking against the chipped linoleum floor. "Not exactly what I was looking for with the insight brew."

Claire almost choked on her tea. "The insight brew?"

"Sage, verbena . . . you know." He waved a hand in the air. "Standard stuff. I use it all the time. Always sleep with it under my pillow. You never know when insight will strike or which direction it'll come from." He shook his head. "But I have to say, I wasn't real happy to see you and old Max show up in my nightmares."

Claire's felt a chill enter the room with the man's name. "Max?"

"Maximilian Constantin." His eyes grew wise as he surveyed them. "You know who I'm talking about."

"Just to clarify," Xander said. "Who, exactly, have you been seeing with the insight spell? Claire?"

Eddie took another drink of his tea. "Not just her. You, too."

"Me?"

Eddie nodded.

"Would you mind telling me what you see?"

"Would you mind telling me what you're looking for?" Eddie asked coolly.

Claire glanced at Xander before answering. She thought about the best way to present everything to Eddie. "Someone placed an order for panther plasma last week."

"I take it Max is this someone?" Eddie asked.

"We think so. I mean, he didn't actually place the order," Claire explained. "But we think he's the one who requisitioned it."

Eddie nodded calmly.

"You don't seem surprised," Xander observed.

"I'm not."

Claire wanted to ask him why, but she doubted he would answer.

"The timing's weird because some of the Guild houses have been broken into recently," she continued.

"And by the houses," Eddie said, "I take it you mean the residences, not the stores."

Claire nodded. "How did you know?"

He shrugged.

"Anyway," Claire continued, "we don't know anything about Maximilian. No one talks about him, not even to make jokes like they do with—" She stopped herself.

Eddie raised one eyebrow, a twinkle of humor in his eyes. "With me?"

At first, Claire didn't say anything. Then, because he seemed to know anyway, she nodded reluctantly.

A thread of bitterness ran through his chuckle. "I'm not surprised."

"What do you mean?" Xander asked.

Eddie leaned forward, lacing his hands together, his eyes bright and intense. "Leaving the Guild is a big deal, young man. You must know it more than anyone."

Xander stiffened. "Why would I know it better than anyone?"

Eddie leaned back. "Come on. I know you. You're Estelle and Bernard's son. The Guild is who you *are*. You know how it is. No one leaves. Not on their own. It's like . . . Well, it's like turning your back on your own blood. Believe me, I know."

"But you didn't leave on your own," Claire said softly. "They . . . Well, they kicked you out." She was embarrassed to say it out loud.

He looked into her eyes. "That what they tell you?"

"It's true, isn't it?" Claire asked.

He regarded her quietly, his eyes solemn.

"You're saying you left voluntarily?" Xander asked. "Why would you do that?"

"Same reason you're here," Eddie said. "Maximilian Constantin."

Xander sat up straighter. "You knew him."

"Everyone in the Guild knew him. Until he left. Then everyone pretended not to."

"Would you mind telling us what happened?" Claire asked.

Eddie thought about it. "It's not a pretty story. And it's not over yet."

"That's okay," Claire said. "We just need to know so we can . . . I don't know, try to protect ourselves."

It took Eddie a minute to start talking. When he did, his voice was slower, like it was moving through a thick haze of memory.

"Max wasn't always part of the New Orleans Guild. He showed up sometime in the nineteen nineties with his daughter."

"His daughter?" Claire couldn't have been more surprised. Maximilian had grown to fairy-tale proportions in her mind. A nefarious villain, complete with a black cape and sinister laugh.

Being a father didn't fit her image of him at all.

"Elisabeta," Eddie said softly. "She was sick. I can't remember with what. Something that put her in a wheelchair. Max had already been ostracized from the Guild in Romania for trying black magic to cure her."

The words came to Claire through a long tunnel.

Something that put her in a wheelchair.

She saw the little girl at the party in her dream, her long dark braids trailing down the back of a wheelchair, Maximilian's face clenched with silent rage as Claire's father took the picture.

"Ah," Eddie said softly. "You've seen her."

Xander glanced sharply at her. When she didn't say anything, Eddie continued.

"Anyway, Max was petitioning New Orleans for permission to use black magic to save Elisabeta. They wouldn't agree, of course. The Guild never bends their rules, even to save a life."

"So what happened?" Xander asked.

"Well, the Guild was in an uproar while Max was here. He was . . . volatile. Enraged by the Guild's refusal to let him try the magic."

"Why didn't he try it on his own?" Claire asked, feeling unexpected sympathy for the man who was trying to save his daughter.

"Couldn't get the supplies, I expect," Eddie said simply. "You know how it is. The Guild's got a lock on anything even remotely exotic, and there are always exotic ingredients in black magic."

She thought about the vial of panther blood in the valise and wondered how Maximilian had gotten ahold of it.

"Max finally left," Eddie continued, "presumably to try and save Elisabeta through the help of an underground branch or with ingredients he found on the black market. But he made a promise on his way out."

"What kind of promise?" Claire whispered.

"Max swore that if Elisabeta died, the Guild would pay."

"And did she?" Claire asked.

"That's what I heard," said Eddie.

"What did all this have to do with you?" Xander asked.

"Let's just say the Guild and I had differing views on its objectives."

"Can you be more specific?" Claire asked.

Eddie regarded her solemnly before speaking again. "I thought Max was a wake-up call."

Xander raised his eyebrows in question. "A wake-up call?"

"We all knew there were people in the community

practicing black magic," he explained. "Always have been. Always will be. It's harder for them without the Guild supply houses. But where there's a will there's a way. I believed the Guild should be more aggressive, more . . . *proactive* about addressing those kinds of threats."

"Threats like Max," Claire said.

Eddie nodded. "But the Guild didn't see it that way. They've been sitting in their big houses too long, holding so-called rituals in air-conditioned rooms, taking shortcuts in their potions and spells when it suits them." He leveled his gaze at Claire and Xander. "Neglecting to properly train and arm the next generation."

Claire felt the hot flush of guilt touch her cheeks.

"So what happened?" Xander asked.

"The way I saw it, we only had two choices: use the craft to bring Max under control or look over our shoulders forever."

Claire shook her head. "But what if you were wrong? What if Max never got the ingredients he needed? What if he changed his mind? Why renounce the Guild for something that may never even happen?"

Eddie didn't say anything for a minute, just rubbed at the condensation dripping down his glass.

"You ever been around a Houngan priest?" he finally asked. "And I mean the real deal, not these fakes you see online now."

Claire remembered the strange vibration she felt around Max, the air so full of darkness it felt heavy, laden with dangerous, evil things.

She shrugged.

"She doesn't believe," Xander explained.

Eddie let out a laugh that sounded more like a cackle. "That's ironic."

"What do you mean?" Claire asked him.

He lowered his voice. "You're Marie's kin. You're more powerful than any of them. You just haven't figured it out yet."

The words seemed to echo through the tiny kitchen. Claire hurried to change the subject.

"You were asking us if we'd even been around a Houngan?"

Eddie nodded. "Max was the real deal. A genuine Houngan with the power to summon the most powerful loas—dark, light, all of them."

Claire should have been surprised. Calling on the assistance of the loas—the spirit beings said to aid practitioners of voodoo in their spells, potions, and ceremonies—was something she'd never believed in. Sure, everyone in the Guild did it, from the leadership right down to everyday people who purchased supplies.

But Claire had always thought of it as a meaningless ritual. Like saying amen after a prayer or asking God to help you, when the truth was, there was no way to be sure anyone was even listening.

Yet somehow, she wasn't at all surprised to hear that Max could summon the loas, wasn't even surprised that she believed he *could*. Max seemed bigger than all of them, and Eddie suddenly seemed like a more reliable witness than anyone in the Guild.

"And that was unusual?" Xander asked. "That kind of power?"

Eddie nodded. "Still is, my man. Still is."

"What does all of this have to do with your decision to leave the Guild?" Claire asked.

"Max's need to save Elisabeta was toxic. It polluted the air around him until you could feel it, like a thundercloud that followed him wherever he went. Petitioning the Guild for permission to use black magic was just a way to gain access to the ingredients he needed. But everyone knew it was a formality. He was already trying to work the spells on his own. Those of us with a sensitivity to the dark side of our craft could feel it on him." He paused.

"Max was the only Houngan who ever truly scared me, and my family's been in voodoo for almost two hundred years. When Max said he'd get his revenge on the Guild families, I didn't doubt it, and without the Guild's permission to use black magic to bring him under control, there was nothing to stop him. The way I saw it, Max was just the beginning. If the Guild wasn't prepared to address a threat like him, who's to say there wouldn't be bigger and badder threats later on?" He shook his head. "There was no upside to staying with the Guild and a whole lot of downside, so I left. The craft's a part of my life. I can take or leave the Guild. One is not dependent on the other."

Claire wondered if she would be as nonchalant as Eddie if the Guild ceased to be a part of her life. Of course, Xander and Sasha would always be her friends. Her parents would always love her. But what about everyone else?

"So why do they . . ." Claire paused, not sure how to pose her question.

He laughed. "Why do they call me Crazy Eddie?"

She smiled, nodding.

"The easiest way to make sure no one follows my example is to cast me as a nutcase. I'll bet a few high-ranking people called me crazy a couple of times and the Guild gossip mill took it and ran with it." He laughed again. "Damn! I'm probably a legend now, am I right?"

Claire smiled again. "Kind of."

Eddie nodded, his voice growing serious. "Max has to be dealt with. You do know that, right?"

He was right, but they couldn't exactly fight Max, using the craft or anything else, if they didn't know what he had in mind, and it's not like they could call the police and demand they arrest him for maybe casting evil spells.

Even if they caught him in the act, voodoo wasn't a crime.

As if he could read her mind, Xander answered. "We're working on it. But the Guild isn't going to be any help."

"You ask them about it?"

Xander shook his head. "Not in so many words, but I think it's safe to say they're not going to change anytime soon. Not even to deal with Max."

"So what's the plan?"

Xander sighed. "We don't have one. Not really. Except . . ." He shot Claire a look.

"Except?" Eddie prodded.

"We found some things," Claire said. "In the house they're staying in."

"In the house they're staying in?" Admiration flashed in Eddie's eyes. "Well, well, well. Seems this litter of firstborns might have some teeth. So are we done?" He leaned forward. "Or are you going to fill me in?"

TWENTY-TWO

Claire told him all about the house on Dauphine, the travel itineraries, the pictures of the Guild firstborns, the letters, and the panther blood. Then she told him about the old photograph and the dream she'd had with the insight potion, the little girl she could only assume was Elisabeta staring balefully into the camera, as if she was watching her own death in its lens.

Eddie was silent for a good minute before he spoke. "These letters . . . Do you have them with you?"

Claire shook her head. "I left them at home."

It had never occurred to her that Eddie would be so normal, let alone that he would be able to help them decode the letters.

He nodded, deep in thought. "You planning on telling the Guild what you're up to?"

"We haven't decided," Xander said.

"We figured it would be best to get as much information as we can first. It'll be harder for them to blow us off if we already know everything," Claire added.

"I can't say that I disagree," Eddie said. He was opening his mouth to say something else when a raspy, demanding voice sounded from the front of the house.

"Eddie? Is it time for my pills?"

It was Miss Thelma, calling to Eddie from the front porch.

Eddie glanced down at the old watch that encircled his left wrist. "Excuse me a minute."

Claire watched Eddie leave the room, waiting until she heard the screen door slam to turn to Xander.

"I think we should ask him to help us."

"Who? Eddie?" Xander asked.

"Think about it," she said. "He was part of the Guild so he knows how things work, but he's just as frustrated as we are with it."

Xander raised his eyebrows. "'We?'"

Claire sighed. "Yes, 'we.' Just because I don't believe in voodoo doesn't mean I don't care about stopping someone like Max. Call it whatever you want, but Eddie's right; the Guild could put a stop to it when they hear about someone like Max, and they don't. I may not be a fan of the Guild, but if they're going to be around, they'd be better off listening to people like Eddie and Allegra when it comes to dealing with crazies like Max."

"Okay, but what would we need Eddie to do, exactly?"

"I think we should ask *him* what to do next. Maybe we need a fresh perspective. Someone who's not so close to it all. And who knows? His background on Max could come in handy, too." She remembered something. "Speaking of which, you haven't asked him about your mom."

Xander's eyes darkened. "I'm getting to it."

"All right, then, Aunt Thelma," Eddie was saying. "You just sit there with your tea. I'll be out to check on you when the young people leave."

The screen door slammed again. Eddie's footsteps grew louder as he came nearer to the kitchen.

Claire looked into Xander's eyes. "So?"

He only hesitated a minute. "Okay."

"Sorry about that," Eddie said, re-entering the kitchen and taking his seat. "Aunt Thelma likes to pretend she doesn't remember anything, but she keeps me on my toes. Now where were we?"

"I just had one more question. About Max." Claire heard the strain in the too-casual tone of Xander's voice.

"Was he . . . involved with anyone while he was here? Anyone from the Guild?"

"What? Romantically?" Eddie shook his head. "Not a chance. Max was too busy trying to save Elisabeta. He didn't have time for tomcatting. In fact, I'd say he was as straight as a monk. Except for that black magic thing."

The relief was visible on Xander's face.

Eddie looked puzzled by the question but let it go. "Anything else I can do for you two?"

Claire glanced at Xander, wanting to make sure he hadn't changed his mind about Eddie, before she spoke again.

"Actually, we were kind of hoping you would be willing to help us figure this all out."

Eddie's nod was slow. "I was kind of hoping you'd ask."

⁂

"Did you have the right address for Crazy Eddie?" Sasha asked as soon as they sat down at their usual table.

It took Claire a minute to reconcile the image that automatically came to mind when someone said "Crazy Eddie" with the reasoned, intelligent person she and Xander had met in Treme.

"No," Claire said. "But he'd only moved a few blocks."

"So you found him?"

Claire nodded.

"What was he like?" Sasha asked.

"Not what we expected," Xander said.

Allegra looked confused. "What do you mean? The guy's a legend."

"He's . . . normal," Claire said.

"Normal?"

Claire shrugged. "Yeah."

"Then why was he kicked out of the Guild?" Sasha asked.

"He wasn't kicked out," Claire said. "He left."

"Why would he do that?" Allegra asked. "Why would anyone?"

"Because of Maximilian."

"Wait . . ." Allegra looked confused. "What does Max have to do with Crazy Eddie leaving the Guild?"

Claire and Xander filled them in. Claire was glad to set the record straight about Eddie after the Guild's hatchet job on his character. Sasha and Allegra would find out the truth soon anyway, but in some strange way, Claire felt like she owed it to Eddie to come to his defense.

"So Maximilian's back to get revenge on the Guild,"

Sasha said quietly. "It's kind of sad, when you think about it. About his daughter."

"I know what you're saying," Xander said. "But it's hard to be sad for the guy when he's breaking into our houses and planning to hex us all."

"You know what I mean. Elisabeta was his *daughter.* Are you saying you wouldn't use the craft to save someone you love? Even if the Guild forbade it?"

Xander's eyes slid to Claire. "I don't know," he admitted.

"So Crazy Eddie—" Allegra started.

"I don't think we should call him that anymore," Claire interrupted. "He's not crazy."

Allegra sighed. "Whatever. The point is, he agreed with me. Even back then, he thought the Guild should be doing more with their power."

Claire nodded. "Yep."

"Did he have any idea what Max might be up to? What he might do to get back at the Guild?"

"We didn't get that far," Xander said. "But you can ask him yourself."

Sasha frowned. "What do you mean? How would we do that?"

"Easy." Xander turned to the window, tapping on it

until Eddie, standing outside the Cup, turned to him with a nod. Xander waved him in. "Like that."

Sasha and Allegra watched dumbfounded through the window as Eddie made his way into the Cup. He cut an imposing figure as he maneuvered his way through the crowd to their table.

Xander and Claire stood up.

"Eddie" —Xander gestured to the two girls— "Sasha Drummond and Allegra St. Martin. Allegra and Sasha, meet Eddie Clement."

TWENTY-THREE

"Now what?" Sasha asked.

It had taken ten minutes for Sasha and Allegra to lose the look of shock on their faces and another twenty for Eddie to answer their questions. A lot of it was a repeat of what Claire and Xander told them when they'd first arrived, but Allegra and Sasha wanted to hear it straight from Eddie. He didn't seem to mind.

"I stopped to pick up the letters so Eddie could read them, too," Claire finally said. She reached into her bag. "Maybe he'll be able to tell us what they have to do with Max and Eugenia."

Claire handed the letters to Eddie and sat back, watching as his eyes skimmed the pages. Xander tapped his fingers impatiently on the table while Sasha and Allegra eyed Eddie with thinly veiled curiosity.

Finally, Eddie looked up, his eyes shaded with concern.

"Well? Do you know what they mean?" Claire asked.

Eddie looked nervously around the Cup before returning his eyes to them. "We can't talk about this here."

∼ℓ∼

They decided to go to the library on Carrolton. For a New Orleans library, voodoo research wasn't exactly out of the norm. It was the closest they could come to a place where they could talk freely.

They entered through the glass doors, making their way past the main desk to one of the empty tables near the back.

Once they were settled, Eddie pulled out the letters he'd been carrying since they left the Cup.

"I'm assuming you've all read these," he said, looking at each of them.

They nodded.

"We get the gist of it," Claire said. "This woman named Sorina wanted revenge for something that happened to her parents. So she contacted Marie and asked for information about some kind of black magic spell called Cold Blood."

"Except Marie shut her down, because, duh, Marie didn't approve of black magic," Allegra continued.

"But she must have tried spells out on her own,"

Claire said. "Otherwise, why would the Guild expel her?"

"That's what I don't get," Sasha said. "Why would Sorina even need Marie's spell? If Sorina knew the craft, couldn't she just create one of her own?"

"She could," Eddie said. "But it would be like baking bread without a recipe. Could you do it and come up with something approximating bread? Maybe. But even if it worked, it probably wouldn't be as good as something tried and true."

"He's right," Allegra agreed. "And the spells for black magic are trickier than most." She sighed. "Come on, Sash. You know this."

Sasha looked offended. "This is . . . you know. Technical stuff. I know what ingredients to mix together for which spells and I remember most of the words for conjuring, but don't ask me about all the rules. I don't pay attention to that kind of thing."

Eddie snorted.

"What?" Allegra said.

He leaned forward, keeping his voice low. "This is what I've been saying; the Guild hasn't prepared you for this kind of attack. They expose you to the craft—and all kinds of people who practice it—and don't teach you to defend yourselves. To defend your families and the

Guild." He made a sound that clearly expressed his exasperation. "It's negligence, plain and simple."

"That's what *I've* been saying!" Allegra crowed, looking at Eddie like he was her new best friend.

Eddie shook his head. "Do they bother training you at all? Teach you ways to make your recipes stronger? Show you how to build your own spells? To figure out where your gifts lie?"

"Our parents teach us stuff when we're little," Sasha said. "Like . . . which ingredients go into which spell and stuff."

"Ingredients," Eddie repeated, disbelieving. "Well, that's one way to handle training, but it's not going to get you very far with someone like Max."

"I guess, in eighteen eighty if you wanted a foolproof spell for black magic, Marie would have been the one to go to," Claire said, trying to turn the conversation back to the letters. It's not that she didn't agree with Eddie and Allegra. But they had more immediate problems than the Guild's training practices and its relevance in modern society.

"In any year," Xander corrected her. "I mean, not to brag, but the Toussaints are pretty well known for the strength of our spells. But they don't hold a candle to Marie's, even after all these years."

"So let's get this straight," Sasha said. "Sorina wanted Marie's spell for revenge, but Marie wouldn't give it to her."

"Right," Xander said. "But Sorina had an idea of what was required, and she kept experimenting until she got it right."

"And the Guild disavowed her," Claire said softly. "Just like Maximilian."

"Except unlike Sorina, Maximilian never mastered the black magic spell he needed," Eddie reminded them. "Not in time anyway. Elisabeta died."

"Well, I think it's safe to say that he mastered something. Otherwise, why would he be here targeting the Guild?" Allegra asked.

Claire reached for the letters, dropping her eyes to the slanted writing. She flipped through the pages, searching for a paragraph in the final letter.

"This is the part I don't understand." She lowered her voice as she recited the words. "*It was never my intention that my spells and potions be used for ill. I have uncovered keys to the craft's darkest door only to foil those with a less altruistic view of it, hoping to have some defense should it be used as a means to harm others. It is a heavy burden to know that my attempts at safeguarding the world from those who would use the craft for evil have instead caused that evil to be unleashed.'"* Claire looked at Eddie. "It almost sounds like the Cold Blood spell was Marie's to start with."

Eddie nodded. "It probably was."

Xander shook his head. "That doesn't make sense. Like Allegra said, Marie didn't condone the use of black magic."

"You know how doctors develop vaccines?" Eddie asked them. "For diseases and such?"

"Sure," Xander said. "They use a weakened or dead form of the microbe that causes the disease to create a kind of antidote."

"In other words, you have to understand the disease to create a cure," Eddie said.

"Wait a minute . . ." Claire said. It was starting to come together. "You're saying Cold Blood was Marie's spell, but she only created it as a way to make a counterspell in case someone else discovered it?"

"Can't fight what you don't know," Eddie said.

Claire was beginning to see his point.

She sighed, turning her attention back to the final letter. "That leaves this then: *'I can only appeal to the all-powerful loas to accept an addendum to the Cold Blood spell. One that will require an ingredient you will never obtain.'"* She looked at Eddie. "What does it mean?"

"A lot of practitioners—especially the old school ones—believe a spell or recipe is only as good as its endorsement by the loas."

Allegra laughed. "You're saying we can create a spell but if the loas don't approve it, it won't work?"

Eddie's nod was slow. "That's what some people believe."

Claire thought about it. "So if Marie believed her original Cold Blood spell had been blessed by the loas and she wanted to make a change so no one else could use it, she would have to ask them to accept the change to the recipe?"

"That's about right," Eddie said.

"One that will require an ingredient you will never obtain," Claire murmured.

"I wonder what the ingredient was," Sasha said. "And if it was enough to stop Sorina."

"I think we're asking the wrong question," Allegra said.

Sasha raised her eyebrows. "What's the right question?"

"Whether Max somehow got ahold of the addendum to Cold Blood. Whether he's planning to use it on the firstborns." She paused, her eyes wide with fear. "On us."

Silence stretched between them. Claire wondered if she was the only one who felt Marie as a palpable presence, as if she were looking over their shoulders, encouraging them to figure out the mystery of Cold Blood. To save themselves.

"It's the only thing that makes sense," Claire finally said. "Why else would Max have the letters? Why else would he take pictures of the firstborns and break into their houses?"

"They're making doll babies," Xander said softly. "Preparing to hex us with the Cold Blood spell as revenge for Elisabeta's death."

"Now you're thinking," Eddie said.

"What about Claire?" Sasha asked. "Why wasn't her picture on the wall? Why hasn't her house been broken into?"

Xander shrugged. "I don't know. Maybe they hadn't taken her picture yet. Maybe she's last."

Allegra turned to Eddie. "Have you ever heard of Cold Blood? Is there a counter?"

Eddie shook his head. "I've heard talk, but like a lot of the old recipes, it's difficult to know how much of it is just legend. And if Marie did create a counter as the letters seem to indicate, I have no idea where we'd find it."

"Can we come up with one on our own?" Allegra asked.

"Without the original spell, it'd be almost impossible," Eddie answered.

"Well, we need to figure something out," Xander said.

He didn't have to say what they were all thinking; his house had already been broken into. Once Maximilian and Eugenia got ahold of something belonging to Sasha—and maybe Claire—whatever they had planned would be set into motion.

"We could talk to the other firstborns," Allegra offered. "Except for Daniel. He's too young. But we could let Charlie and William and Laura in on everything and see if they have any ideas. Laura's really talented with recipes. Maybe she could try to develop something."

Claire shook her head. "I don't want to do that."

"Why not? Because you don't trust them?" Allegra asked, her blue eyes looking into Claire's. "They're just like us."

Claire tried to think of a way to explain that wouldn't sound offensive. "It's nothing personal. I just don't know them very well, that's all."

Allegra shrugged. "Whose fault is that?"

"Allegra . . ." There was a subtle warning in Xander's voice.

"I'm just saying," Allegra continued, turning her attention back to Claire, "the other firstborns are there. They'd help if they knew we needed it."

"I don't know." Xander tapped his fingers along the edge of the table. "Maybe we should just take it to the Guild."

"No way." Claire was as surprised by her vehemence as Xander. "They made Eddie out to be some kind of nut job just to keep their secret. I don't trust them to tell us anything at this point. We could give them what we have and they could just pat us on the head and tell us to let them take care of everything. For all we know, that would be the last we heard of it, ever."

"Would that be so bad?" Xander asked. "At least someone would be taking care of it. Someone who knows what we're up against."

Eddie chuckled softly. They stopped arguing, turning to where he sat, his expression as placid as the Pontchartrain on a windless summer day.

Xander scowled. "What's so funny?"

"You," Eddie said with a smile. "The fact that you

still believe the Guild knows *anything* about what it's up against."

"Well, they may not be doing much about black magic in our ranks, but they definitely know more than we do," Xander said.

"You're right about that, my man. And that's just the way they want it," Eddie said. "Question is: How long do *you* want it to be that way?"

The words hung between them.

"Eddie has a point," Sasha said. "Our parents might know more than we do, but that's not saying much. I mean, it seems to me that they've made a pretty big mess of things. Not to mention the fact that, based on what Eddie told you, the Guild knew Max could pose a threat all this time. But they never said a word about it, and from the looks of things, they didn't do anything about it either."

Allegra nodded. "Exactly. And anyway, each new generation in the Guild has to step up at one point or another," she added. "The older generation becomes, well, old or tired or ineffective and—"

"Hey, now . . ." Eddie protested.

She smiled at him. "There are exceptions. I'm just say-ing that maybe it's time for us to stop letting our parents take care of everything. Maybe it's time we step up and start *acting* like firstborns."

"There's just one problem," Xander said. "We don't have any idea what we're dealing with."

"Right," Sasha agreed. "We can't even start looking for a counterspell until we know what the Cold Blood spell does."

Allegra leaned in, lowering her voice to a whisper. "Let's think about this; if it's used on someone's enemies, it has to be a spell to kill someone in cold blood or with cold blood or . . ."

"By turning their blood cold," Claire tried.

The words sat between them.

"We can't be sure exactly what it is," Sasha said. "And it's not like we have time to experiment with counterspells in the hopes that we stumble on the right one."

"I might be able to help with that."

They turned to Eddie.

"You guys up for a drive?"

TWENTY-FOUR

They piled into Eddie's car, Xander in front, the three girls in the back. It didn't take Claire long to realize they were heading back into Treme.

After about half an hour, they turned onto North Claiborne. The highway loomed overhead, blocking out the sun on one side of the street. A row of run-down shops lined the other. Eddie parked next to the curb in front of an old building. The structure itself had seen better days, but the red paint job was fresh, the sidewalk swept, the windows gleaming.

For the first time in days, Claire had the urge to take a picture. Too bad she'd left her camera at home when she and Xander had left for Treme. Was it really just this morning?

Eddie got out of the car.

"What is this place?" Claire asked, stepping out into the heat.

"The only one I can think of that might have an answer about the Cold Blood spell," Eddie said, leading the way to the bright blue door.

They followed him inside and were immediately plunged into cooler air scented with incense. Claire caught sandalwood, patchouli, frankincense. The light was dim, and she reached out for Xander, touching his arm as she waited for her eyes to adjust. Sasha and Allegra came in behind them and shut the door.

"Be right there." The voice was slightly husky and came from somewhere beyond the front of the cluttered room. It was followed by the sound of shuffled paper and the slow drag of something heavy being moved across the floor.

Sasha and Claire shuffled nervously from foot to foot while Xander peered into the dim recesses at the back of the room. Eddie, unfazed, leaned against the wooden counter.

Claire took advantage of the time to look around. They appeared to be in a large storefront, although it wasn't like any store she'd ever seen. Bookshelves lined the walls, and an odd assortment of objects was stacked haphazardly on shelves, tables, even the floor. She recognized some of it: gris-gris bags in various states of disrepair, stained and unraveling dolls, sticks of incense—some of them half burned—standing up in a small vase.

If the Kincaids' supply shop resembled an old-fashioned general store, this place looked like some kind of demented thrift shop. Even after all the years Claire had spent working around voodoo supplies, she couldn't make out any kind of organization in the jumble of objects, most of which seemed old, used, or damaged.

The sound of approaching footsteps drew her eyes to a narrow aisle between shelves leading to the back of the store.

"There! Sorry about that," a woman said, her face and body just a smudge in the shadows. "Seems I never stop having to reorganize!" She stepped into the light cast from an old lamp on an oak table. Claire was surprised at how slight she was, both in height and in build. Her skin was as pale as porcelain, her hair even blonder than Claire's and separated into dreadlocks. Blue eyes skimmed the rest of them before landing on Eddie. She grinned. "Had a feeling I'd be seeing you soon."

He stepped toward her with a sly smile. "Did ya now?"

They embraced and stepped away from each other.

"Therese Charbonnet," he said, gesturing to them with his hand. "This is Xander, Sasha, Allegra, and Claire. Guys, this is a good friend of mine, Therese Charbonnet."

"Nice to meet you." Her eyes rested on Claire. "You're Marie's kin."

Claire nodded.

Therese's eyes lingered on hers before taking in the others and coming back to Eddie. "You're looking for recipes, dark ones, yes?"

"That's right," Eddie said. "Cold Blood."

"Cold Blood?"

"You know it?"

She thought about it. "Not by that name, but that doesn't mean I haven't come across it as something else."

Eddie shrugged. "Don't have much else. We think it was Marie the First's. Could be as far back as the eighteen eighties, although it could also have been reproduced somewhere along the way."

"Wait a minute," Allegra broke in. "How did you—"

"How did I know what you were coming for?" Therese asked.

"Well, yeah. We only showed Eddie the letters a couple of hours ago."

Therese's eyebrows shot up as she regarded Allegra. "I imagine you would be able to figure that out better than anyone else."

Allegra sucked in her breath. "You see things? Before they happen?"

Therese hesitated. "Sometimes. And sometimes I just *know.*"

Allegra couldn't stop staring at her, and for the first time, it occurred to Claire that maybe she wasn't the only one who'd been feeling alone. Being a part of the Guild, really a part of it, and even knowing your place in it obviously didn't guarantee smooth sailing. If Allegra was the only one of the firstborns with true psychic ability, it had to freak her out at least a little. And if her parents were as close-lipped about her gifts as the Guild was about everything else, she probably hadn't gotten a lot of guidance. Judging from the look on her face, she had plenty of questions.

"So!" Therese looked around the shop. "Welcome to

my humble abode. I'm sure it isn't up to Guild Code, but we do have things here that can't be found anywhere else. No guarantees you'll find what you're looking for, but let's see what we can do. Follow me."

She led them toward the back of the store. They passed tables and shelves, all groaning with the weight of so much stuff that Claire wondered if it was going to fall on top of them any minute.

"What exactly is this place?" Sasha said.

Therese's laugh was musical as they rounded a corner at the back of the store and entered another room. "I call it the orphanage."

"The orphanage?" Xander repeated.

"Yep." She ushered them into the room. The walls were lined with books, the room separated into four equal spaces by yet more shelves. "I collect relics, books, historical accounts, recipes, antiques . . . anything related to the craft."

Xander looked around. "Where do you get it all?"

"Estate sales, local thrift stores, yard sales, and online auction sites," she said. "Anywhere I can."

"You mean anywhere *we* can," Eddie said.

Therese nodded. "Right. Eddie . . . subsidizes my efforts."

Sasha looked around. "So this isn't a Guild-sanctioned store."

Therese laughed. "You could say that. Then again, the Guild isn't really interested in what we do."

"But why collect all this stuff?" Claire asked, looking from Eddie to Therese. "What are you going to do with it all?"

"Use it, we hope," Eddie answered.

"You're collecting it to ward off black magic," Allegra said softly.

"That's part of it," Eddie said. "But we're also trying to preserve the history of the craft before it gets water-logged in the next hurricane or lost in a fire or thrown out with the trash. There's a lot to be learned from the old ways. Even the doll babies were wrapped differently back in the old days. For all we know those kinds of things make a difference in the strength and purity of a spell. But you're right; having weapons in the arsenal to deal with threats like Max is a big part of our motivation."

"So if the Guild won't take care of it, you will?" Claire suggested.

He gave her a slow nod, his expression grave. "Something like that."

She was still thinking about that when Eddie spoke to Therese. "So what's our best bet? The wall by the window? Or have you moved everything around again?"

"I had to reorganize last week when a new batch of books came in from an estate in the bayou. Let's see . . ." She looked around, like she was trying to remember where she put everything. "Let's start with that shelf, there." She pointed to a shelf against the wall. "If that doesn't work. It's anybody's guess."

Eddie sighed. "Okay, let's get to it."

He assigned them each shelves, and they took seats wherever they could find them. Claire started at the halfway point, planning to work her way down while Xander worked his way up from the same shelf.

"What exactly are we looking for?" Therese said from the other end of the shelf.

"We don't really know." Eddie pulled a book covered in tattered green cloth from the shelf and opened it. "We found mention of it in an old letter, but there weren't any ingredients and there wasn't anything specific about what it does."

"Maybe we should pull anything having to do with blood," Therese suggested. "We can go through them all when we're done and see what we've got."

"That works," Eddie said.

For a while they were silent, lost in the never-ending supply of books, the musty smell of old pages, and the words of long-dead Mambo Priestesses and Houngan Priests. An hour later, Sasha looked up from a book in her lap.

"Not gonna lie; some of this stuff's starting to creep me out."

"I know what you mean," Allegra said. "I had no idea most of these recipes even existed."

"If they're even real," Xander said.

"So you're telling me, you believe in the craft's ability to heal and protect but not to do harm?" Eddie asked him.

Xander thought about it. "I don't know. It just seems too . . . out there, you know?"

"No, I don't know," Eddie said, firmly closing the book in his hands and leaning forward in his metal chair. "Where do you think modern voodoo came from? Why do you think that in a world that demands a scientific explanation for everything, people still turn to the craft?"

Xander shrugged. "Why do they turn to religion? I mean, I may believe in God, but that doesn't mean I believe every single word of the Bible."

"Xander thinks voodoo's power is mostly in the herbology and root work," Claire explained to Eddie and Therese. "Kind of like homeopathic medicine with a little bit of conjured energy stirred in."

"Okay," Eddie said, "but if magic and medicine can mix to make something beneficial, why can't it mix to make something harmful? How is it any different from modern medicine, which can heal, but can also destroy if used in the wrong way?"

"I don't know," Xander admitted. "I guess I haven't given much thought to black magic."

Therese gave a forlorn sigh.

"What?"

"Just . . . you guys are a long way from your roots, that's all."

Xander flushed a little. Claire lowered her eyes back to the book in front of her, wondering why more and more, it seemed Eddie, and now Therese, was the voice of reason.

The light from outside—already minimal when they'd arrived—had faded to gray by the time they finished all the books in the back room. Therese had long since gone back to work at the front of the store. Claire stood up and stretched. She'd made a list on her phone of spells involving blood and had stacked the books containing them on the floor so they wouldn't get mixed back in with the others.

"What did you get?" Eddie asked her.

She looked at her phone. "Something to boil the blood, something to turn it to ash, and one recipe that seemed to stop it from flowing."

"Could that be it?" Xander asked. "I mean, if you turned blood cold enough, it might not move through someone's veins."

"Anything's possible," Eddie said. "But without the original spell or something clearly pointing to Cold Blood, there's no way to know for sure."

"What did you guys find?" Claire asked them.

She listened while they checked their respective lists. Although some of the spells were freaky enough to give Claire chills, nothing came up that could be clearly interpreted as Cold Blood.

Allegra crossed her arms in front of her chest. "Now what? There has to be somewhere else we can look."

Claire realized how surreal her world had become as they all turned to Eddie. Just a few days ago, they had thought he was some crazy Guild outcast. Now he was the only one really helping them.

"Let me talk to Therese," he said. "Maybe she can ask

around some of the more . . . unconventional channels."

"Now *that* sounds intriguing," Allegra said.

"That's one word for it," Eddie said wryly.

Eddie filled Therese in on their failed search, and she agreed do some digging for information on the Cold Blood spell. They said good-bye and headed back to Eddie's car in the twilight, the sun almost completely lost behind the looming overpass.

Claire gazed out the window as they drove back to the Cup to pick up their cars. She thought about the Cold Blood spell, wondering what had happened to it. How could such a powerful spell, one that struck fear even in Marie, just disappear into the vapor of history?

She glanced at Sasha and turned back to the window with her heart in her throat. The Drummonds and hers were the only families left to suffer a break-in.

They were almost out of time.

They parted at the Cup and agreed to touch base the next day. Eddie waited for Sasha and Allegra to drive off before turning to Claire and Xander.

"You be careful now," Eddie said. "And I don't just mean on the drive home."

Claire had one foot in Xander's car when she remembered something. "Eddie?"

"Yeah?"

"You never told us what you were seeing. In your dream about me?"

He didn't say anything for a minute. Then he walked back toward them, stopping when he was right in front of Claire.

He sighed, his eyes dark with regret. "The Houngan was bleeding you. And your blood was being used to kill the others."

TWENTY-FIVE

Claire had dinner with her parents and then went upstairs. She tried to read, but her eyes skimmed over the words, her brain absorbing nothing. She read the same page four times before she gave up and set the book aside.

She lay in the dark, staring at the ceiling and thinking about Marie. The letters left no doubt that at least one version of the Cold Blood spell had been hers.

And yet she'd hidden it well.

Other than rumors, no one had even heard of it. If Therese couldn't find anything out through her mysterious "unconventional channels," the firstborns were in serious trouble.

Claire turned over the possibilities in her mind, grasping at anything that might give them answers. Anywhere the spell might be recorded.

But she came up empty, and after what seemed like forever, she finally got up and walked across the room. She searched the floor around her desk and armoire until she caught a flash of red peeking out from under the wardrobe.

Bending down, she picked up the gris-gris bag she'd thrown across the floor a couple of nights before. She lifted it to her nose, the scent of sage and verbena and the underlying smell of the Solomon's seal chips still strong.

She took it back to her bed and put it under her pillow. Then she lay down, recalling the words to the Insight spell and murmuring them into the darkness.

صلى

Claire moved through the hall, not of her usual house, but of another, smaller home that felt welcoming even though it was unfamiliar.

Candles flickered from the sconces on the wall, frankincense heavy in the air. She followed the smell, coming to a small room off the main hall. Soft golden light reached to her from within. She stepped into the room.

The first thing she noticed was the altar on top of a table in the corner. Candles of every color and several wax dolls sat atop a fringed cloth as the smoke from a stick of incense coiled into the air. The plaster walls were cracked in places, but the room was comfortable and warm with flames emanating heat from the fireplace.

The rustling of paper forced Claire's attention to the writing table against the wall. A woman sat there, long black braids snaking down her back as she bent her head to something on the desk, her hand moving swiftly back and forth. She muttered softly as she wrote.

Claire moved closer, aware that she was dreaming and would not be seen. As soon as she looked over the woman's shoulder, she understood. The woman was writing not on paper, but in a book. Claire recognized the script, both from the letters they'd found and the spell book that felt more familiar than ever.

It was her great-great-grandmother Marie.

She finished her writing with a flourish and stood, leaving the book open on the writing table as she crossed to the altar. Claire caught a glimpse of the page on which she'd been writing.

A Plea to the Loas

Claire wanted to finish reading what was on the page, but Marie commanded her attention as she picked up a chunky dish on top of the altar. She began choosing things from the table, throwing them into the dish so quickly that Claire could barely follow her movements.

She ground the ingredients together before lifting a tiny carafe and tipping it over the stone bowl. A stream of glistening oil poured into the mixture. Marie again mixed everything together before turning to a pewter pitcher, pouring a clear liquid from it into the dish.

When she'd again mixed everything together, she picked a brush up from the table and carried it, together with the stone bowl, back to the writing table.

She sat down and began brushing the mixture over the script. Claire watched in fascination as the words began to fade. Marie was still brushing toward the bottom of the page when the top half disappeared completely.

By the time she leaned back to survey her work, the entire page was blank.

She looked at it with satisfaction, stiffening with some kind of awareness before turning her head in Claire's direction. Her eyes seemed to meet Claire's through the veil that separated them.

Then, very deliberately, she turned back to the book, closing it and leaning back, almost as if she were trying to show Claire the volume in which she'd been working.

The cover was cracked, with a slightly green cast. Despite the faded images—a giant snake winding its way around a twisted vine border and words Claire couldn't quite read—she recognized the book as the one that held Marie's spells. The one that sat, usually undisturbed, in the safe under the counter downstairs.

Marie took the book over to the altar, where she placed it in front of the lit candles. She began to chant words in a language Claire couldn't place, steady and rhythmic, almost as if in time to a silent drumbeat.

Then Claire was pulled back and back, through the halls of the candlelit house, the walls and rooms fading to black around her.

The last thing she heard was Marie's voice, echoing through the darkened halls of her sleep, sending her a message she almost understood.

TWENTY-SIX

She woke up with her heart racing, the dream coming back to her in pieces. The first thing she remembered was the house, then Marie and the ritual in front of the altar.

She sat up and reached for her cell phone.

Ten fifteen a.m.

Jumping out of bed, she hurried down the hall, passing the open door of her parents' bedroom. The bed was made, the room empty.

She continued down the stairs. She needed some time alone in the store, and as she made her way to the kitchen, she was relieved to see a note on the refrigerator where her dad always left them.

WENT WITH MOM ON ERRANDS. HOLD DOWN FORT TILL WE GET BACK. LOVE, DAD

She wasted no time heading for the store. Her dad's

message was clear. He wanted her to man the counter in the store until they got back. But they didn't officially open until eleven, which gave Claire at least a little time to find what she needed.

She started with the oldest reference books they had. Disappearing ink was a tool of the past. If someone wanted to hide something now, there were more sophisticated ways to do it. But a potion to cloak ink made perfect sense for someone in the 1800s.

Especially a voodoo queen who wanted to hide her most important spells.

Or counterspells.

She found the recipe in the third book. It was from the early 1900s, but the handwriting was small and neat, the ink only slightly faded. She ran down the list of ingredients, relieved to see that they had everything in stock.

Moving around the store with a bowl and the book, she started with coral root, rubbing the dried buds between her palms and letting the resulting powder fall into the bowl. She added the stamens of gall-of-the-earth, a delicate flower that looked nothing like its name, and continued with camphor root shavings. There were other things: powders and herbs and dried flowers. She added them all, finishing with two drops each of althaea and yarrow.

Following the instructions in the book, she added a drizzle of oil, blessed by her mother. Some of the stores were renowned for their spells, some for their eclectic inventory, and still others for something as simple as their prices. But many of the Kincaids' most loyal customers came for just a few minutes with Claire's mother and her special oils.

Claire finished the recipe with a long pour of distilled water. Then she put the book down and used a stirring stick to mix everything together. The potion smelled strongly of flowers, the camphor an undercurrent that made her think of cough drops.

She turned to pick up Marie's book, placing it on the counter, open to the final blank pages. Grabbing a brush from the box under the counter, she dredged the bristles through the concoction and brushed it lightly over the first blank page.

It left oily streaks, the dried herbs sticking to the page, the gall-of-the-earth turning it yellow in places. She blew on it, willing the words to coalesce, but after ten minutes, nothing happened and she turned to the next page, repeating the process.

This page, too, was blank. Something twisted in Claire's stomach; the knowledge that if the Cold Blood spell and its counter weren't in Marie's book, they were out of options. They would have to go to the Guild, and they could bet that would be the end of their involvement. The Guild would sweep it under the rug, pat her and Xander and Sasha and Allegra on their heads, and send them on their way. They wouldn't know the truth of what Maximilian was planning.

And they wouldn't know how to stop him.

They would be gambling on the Guild's ability to protect them, something that didn't exactly inspire confidence after everything that had happened.

She was on the last few pages, the mixture getting low as she brushed it across yet another page of the book, when something caught her eye. Looking closer, she wondered if it was her imagination. But no. There *was* something there.

Claire blew on the page and waved it back and forth, hoping whatever was there would become clearer once the page was dry.

It did, but only a little. The script was visible now, a shadow on the paper if she tipped it to the light at just the right angle, but she still couldn't make out the words.

She eyed the mixture in the bowl, wondering if there was enough for one more pass across the paper. Deciding she didn't have a choice, she dipped the brush into the bowl and worked it across the page, careful not to saturate it so much that it tore.

The words became more obvious, the ink darker, as the second coat of the potion covered the page.

Waiting for it to dry was excruciating, but with each minute that passed, the words became clearer. She could almost read them, and she tipped the bowl upside down, wiping out every drop with the brush and working a thin third coat over the page.

It was dry five minutes later. And now she could see.

The handwriting matched the other recipes in the book, the title at the top of the page making the tiny hairs on the back of Claire's neck rise.

A Plea to the Loas

She saw Marie, head bent to the blank pages of the book, in her dream. Claire kept reading.

With consideration that my original potion for Cold Blood, devised only to ensure a cure in the event the recipe is created by others for evil or ill purposes, I, Marie Leveau, do humbly ask the loas—all who have been, who are, and who will yet come—to honor my request of a restriction on the original spell, that henceforth, the spell will require a final ingredient added by me in this dark hour as one among us seeks to work it for evil, causing the blood of her enemies to freeze in the mortal body.

It is my humble plea that the doll babies crafted using personal objects of the intended victim should be immersed in all previously instructed items with the addition of this last:

Blood given by one true and powerful enough to summon and call the loas to her aid.

Once immersion occurs, the ritual may commence as is our custom.

Should my worst fears be realized, the spell discovered by one who would use it to cause harm, those among us with authority of old may conjure a cure by use of the following.

Black Hen Feathers
Patchouli
Black Snakeroot
Adder's Tongue
Asafoetida
Devil Pod

As with the addendum to the original spell, so, too, must the counterspell include it.

Claire read the whole page twice, trying to process what she was seeing. What Marie's words were saying.

But there were only a few that mattered. A few that jumped out at her:

Causing the blood to freeze in the mortal body . . . The doll babies crafted using personal objects of the intended victim . . .

And now she knew for sure what the Cold Blood spell was. Even with all the recipes for black magic that they'd seen at Therese's, even with the evidence staring her in the face, it was hard to imagine someone committing murder by using a voodoo spell to freeze the blood in their veins.

Then there was the addition—one Claire could only assume was Marie's addendum to the original spell. What did it mean by *"blood given by one true and powerful enough to summon and call the loas to her aid?"* Who was true and powerful enough to make such a summons? A Mambo? Or was Marie's use of the pronoun "she" just a product of her time? A nod to an era where the most powerful practitioners of the craft were often Mambo Priestesses?

Claire's cell phone vibrated on the counter. She reached for it absently, her mind still reeling from what she'd discovered. The display said her dad was calling.

She picked up the phone. "Hey, Dad."

"Hey, honey. Listen, Mom and I were heading home when we got a call from Christopher Drummond."

"Sasha's dad?"

"Yes." Warning bells clanged in Claire's mind as her dad hesitated. "I thought you'd want to know the Drummonds' house was broken into early this morning."

She dropped onto the stool. "Is Sasha okay?"

"Everybody's okay," her dad said. "We're on the other side of town, but we can swing by and pick you up on our way if you want. I just assumed you'd want to be there, too."

Claire stood, picking up the book and cleaning up the dusting of coral root on the counter. "No . . . I mean, yes! I want to be there. But don't go out of your way to come get me. I'll ride my bike. I can probably get there before you."

Her dad sighed, his tone turning worried. "I don't

know . . . Maybe I should have Xander come pick you up."

She thought of the black Rover, the feeling that someone was always following her, always watching her.

But it didn't matter. Sasha needed her. And Claire wanted to get to her as fast as possible. She would keep to the more populated streets and be vigilant for anyone on her tail.

"It's fine, Dad. It's not that far. I've ridden to Sasha's a hundred times."

He didn't speak for a few seconds and she knew he was thinking about it. "Okay, but text me if you beat us there."

"I will." She was already on her way up the stairs. "See you soon."

Claire hung up the phone and stopped at the top of the stairs to lock the door. She hadn't thought to ask her dad about the store, but it would just have to stay closed until they got back.

She texted Sasha on her way to her room.

JUST HEARD. ARE YOU OKAY???

She was brushing her teeth when her phone lit up from the bathroom counter.

FINE. OK, NOT FINE. FREAKED OUT.

Claire rinsed her mouth before answering. ON MY WAY. BE THERE IN 25.

She was halfway down the hall when she realized she'd left Marie's book sitting on the counter in the store. She ran downstairs and stuffed it into her bag.

Then she got her bike and pedaled for the street.

TWENTY-SEVEN

It was about five miles from her house to Sasha's. Not exactly around the block, but not a big deal, either.

She made her way across town, glancing over her shoulder every couple of minutes, watching for the black Rover. But there was nothing unusual, no one following her that she could see.

She pulled into the gates at the front of Sasha's property and worked her way around the cars parked in the driveway. She was easing her bike next to the garage when Pauline Drummond's voice rang out from the balcony at the back of the house.

"Claire!" Claire turned, returning Aunt Pauline's wave. Claire could see the worry on her face despite the fact that she was as pulled together as ever, her dark hair pulled into a sleek bun. "Let yourself in, honey. It's so sweet of you to come."

Sasha was in the kitchen when Claire entered through the back door.

"Hey!" Claire rushed over, giving her a hug. She was surprised to feel Sasha—tough, stoic Sasha—shaking. She pulled back to look at her friend. "You okay?"

Sasha nodded. "I think so. I mean, you know, I'm upset. But nobody was hurt, so that's good. Everyone's upstairs. Uncle Bernard sent over his security guys to take a look around."

Claire sat down on one of the chairs that faced the eat-in counter. She pulled Sasha into the chair next to her.

"Did they take anything?" she asked softly.

"Not that we can see."

Claire exhaled, panic building inside her like a wave. "Well, don't worry. I found the Cold Blood spell."

Sasha shook her head. "Are you kidding? Because I'm really not—"

"I'm not kidding," Claire stopped her. "And that's not all. The counterspell was with it."

Sasha's eyes were wide. "Claire . . ."

"Thank God," Xander's voice interrupted their conversation. He came into the room, his face flushed as he looked at Claire. "Don't you ever check your phone? I've been texting you for the last half hour."

Claire blinked in surprise. "Um . . . I've been a little busy."

Xander sighed, stepping closer to her and pulling her against him. "I'm sorry. I was worried. I didn't want you to ride your bike. I was going to pick you up on my way."

"It's okay. I was in a hurry to get here. I didn't think to look at my phone once I left the house." She remembered her conversation with her dad. "Speaking of which, I take it my parents aren't here yet?"

Sasha shook her head. "Not that I know of."

Claire texted her dad to let him know she'd arrived safely. When she was done, Sasha turned to Xander.

"She found the Cold Blood spell. And the counter was with it."

"Wait . . ." Xander said. "What?"

Claire pulled the book out of her bag.

"Is that what I think it is?" Sasha asked reverently.

Claire nodded, suddenly feeling shy about it. "Yeah."

"Can I . . . ?" Sasha reached for it.

"Sure." Claire pushed it toward her.

Sasha turned the pages, skimming the recipes. "I remember when you let me look at this for the first time. What were we? Five?" She laughed. "Your mom got so mad. She snatched it away faster than I could say Devil's Pod. I've been dying for another look ever since."

"Well, you can look at it all you want later." She pulled the book toward her and turned to the back of it. "I had this weird dream last night. I saw a woman, and for some reason, I was sure it was Marie the First. She was writing something in a book. I couldn't see the words very clearly, but she mixed a potion and spread it over them and the ink just . . . disappeared."

"Disappeared?" Xander repeated.

"Yeah, you know, it just . . . faded right in front of my eyes. So this morning I decided to see if maybe something was hidden in Marie's old spell book. It took me a while to find an uncloaking recipe, but I finally found it in one of the wartime books. You know the ones with the—"

"Wait a second," Sasha said, a smile beginning to turn her mouth up at the corners. "Are you saying that you, Claire Kincaid, unbeliever of all unbelievers, used the *craft* to get this ink to appear?"

Claire sighed. "Can we please not make a big deal out of it? Because I have a lot of stuff to tell you."

Sasha's grin made her look more like her usual self

than she had since Claire had arrived. "Sure. Go ahead. But we're not done talking about this."

"Whatever," Claire said, rolling her eyes. "Anyway, I followed the recipe and mixed up the potion. At first, nothing happened, and I thought I got it wrong, but then I came to this." She opened it to the Cold Blood addendum and its counterspell, half expecting the words to be gone.

They were right where she left them.

"What the hell . . . ?" Xander murmured, leaning in closer.

"It's the same handwriting as the letters," Sasha said.

"I know. Marie wrote them both, I think. Here." Claire pushed the book toward them. "Read it."

They were silent as they lowered their eyes to the paper. Claire tapped her toes nervously against the tile floor until Sasha looked up.

"Well?" Claire said.

"Maximilian wants to turn our blood cold?"

Claire nodded. "The whole spell isn't there, just the addendum. But I think that's the entire counterspell."

"You can tell a lot about what a recipe requires by its counter," Sasha murmured. "Some of this stuff is standard, but Asafoetida? That's just weird. And what's with the '*blood given by one true and powerful enough to summon and call the loas to her aid*'?"

"I don't know," Claire said. "It's so vague. I was thinking maybe it means a Houngan or Mambo gives their blood to help perform the spell?"

"Man . . ." Sasha muttered. "Voodoo was freaky back then."

"Well, if that's what it means, it sounds like you need the blood for both the Cold Blood spell and its counter," Xander said, studying the page.

"What makes you say that?" Sasha asked.

"'*As with the addendum to the original spell, so, too, must the counterspell include it,*'" he read. "It's saying that the ingredient added to the original spell has to be in the counter, too."

Claire hadn't gotten that far, but it made sense. "So to work the counter, you'd have to have the blood of someone powerful enough to use in the spell, too."

Xander picked up the book. "If this ties into the letters, Sorina's the one Marie was talking about when she wrote 'one among us seeks to work it for evil.'"

"Right," Sasha said. "So she made a plea to the loas that the spell be allowed only with blood from someone powerful enough to summon the loas." She sighed. "Way to be vague, Marie."

"Well, she does use the word 'she' in the addendum," Xander said.

"Maybe Eugenia's a Mambo?" Sasha suggested. "She could be planning to use her own blood in the spell."

Claire shook her head. "I don't think we should rule out men. For all we know, Marie used 'she' as an all-purpose pronoun. I have a feeling Max is way more powerful than Eugenia."

Xander nodded. "That would make sense. He's the one who wants to use the spell against the Guild."

"Against us," Sasha said softly. "As revenge for what happened to Elisabeta."

Now that they were connecting the dots, Claire thought of something. "Maximilian had the letters, but they don't contain the spell. How does he even know what to do if it was such a secret?"

"There was one other book written by Marie," Sasha said softly. "Another spell book."

Claire thought about the book that had been stolen from the Kincaid store. She'd been just a kid when it had happened and hadn't given it much thought, hadn't understood why her father's face had been ashen, her mother near tears.

"You think Maximilian stole it," Claire said softly.

"Which would mean he's been working on this a long time."

"It makes sense," Xander said. "And he wouldn't have bothered with the other book if it looked like a standard spell primer."

"I don't even know if they were together at the time of the theft. We only put the other book in the safe after the first one was stolen."

Sasha was quiet for a minute before she spoke. "Max probably got the letters first. Once he had those, he would know there was such a thing as the Cold Blood spell. Then, all he'd have to do is figure out where the recipe was. And that would have led him back to New Orleans." Sasha looked into Claire's eyes. "Back to you and your family."

"But why would Marie write down such a dangerous spell?" Claire asked.

"Just because she was a Mambo doesn't mean she had the memory to hold thousands of spells in her head," Xander answered.

They were quiet for a minute before Sasha spoke.

"Well, at least we have the counterspell. We can work it up and Maximilian won't be able to do anything to us."

"If we're strong enough," Claire added. "Plus, what

about the other ingredient? The blood given by someone really powerful?"

"The three of us plus Allegra should be able to coun-
teract one voodoo priest," Sasha said. "And we can ask
Eddie what he thinks about the blood. He's old-school.
He has to know someone powerful enough."

"Where are we going to do this?" Xander asked.
"Since we don't have a store on-site, my place is out. We
don't have a work space other than the room upstairs
that my mom uses."

A couple of guys in suits trailed through the kitchen.

"Excuse us," one of them said. Claire recognized him
as one of Bernard's security contingent.

"I think it's safe to say my house is out, too," Sasha
said when the men had exited through the back door.
"Too much going on. Too many people."

"We can use our store," Claire said. "My parents aren't
even here yet. Your parents will want to fill them in on
everything, they'll talk about it forever, and then my parents will want to stick around to make sure yours are okay.
I'd say we have at least a couple of hours, probably more."

"Aren't they expecting you to be here, though?" Sasha
asked.

"I'll tell them we're going back to our house to get

you away from all the activity here. You can tell your parents the same thing. After everything that happened, it makes perfect sense. We can call Allegra and Eddie on the way."

Sasha's nod was slow as she thought about it. "I'll go upstairs and tell my mom and dad."

Xander pulled his keys out of his pocket. "I'll drive."

"I have my bike," Claire reminded him.

"We'll put it in the back. Sasha should still be able to fit back there if she squeezes."

After everything that had happened—everything that *was* happening—Claire wasn't about to argue.

She texted her parents while Sasha was upstairs. When she slipped her phone back into her pocket, Xander took one of her hands.

"You used a de-cloaking spell." He said it softly, like he was afraid that if he made a big deal about it he'd scare her off.

"I guess I did," she admitted.

"So . . . what does that mean?" he asked.

She considered the question, more loaded than it sounded on the surface.

"I don't know," she finally said. "I needed answers. But I haven't had a chance to really think about it."

He nodded, pulling her to him. "That's okay. We have time."

Sasha returned a couple of minutes later. "All set."

"I'll get my bike," Claire said. "I left it out back."

"We'll pull the car up," Xander said. "The driveway was packed. I had to park around the block."

"Meet you guys out front in a couple of minutes."

Sasha and Xander headed for the front of the house while Claire exited through the back. She could hear Bernard's men talking somewhere to the left of the property, probably searching the grounds for clues about how the intruder had gotten in and out without being seen.

She headed for the garage, disengaging the kickstand and rolling her bike down the driveway toward the street.

She couldn't help being nervous about the counterspell. Working a spell in private on the off chance that it would do some good was one thing. Working it in front of others—people who were more skilled and knew more about the craft—when so much was at stake was a lot scarier.

And it would all be for nothing if they couldn't find someone powerful enough to give their blood for the counterspell.

She stopped at the end of the driveway, looking left

and right for Xander's car. He must have had to park a long ways away. He wasn't there yet.

She was reaching into her bag for a piece of gum when she heard his footsteps. "I could have ridden my bike to the—"

Claire barely had time to register the presence of the man, the one who had followed her to the cemetery on the day of the ball.

He was within three feet of her when he opened his palm and blew. A fine dusting of powder escaped his hand, drifting across the space between them, coloring the air gray.

Even as she moved to cover her nose and mouth, she knew she was too late. Some of the craft's most powerful—and dangerous—potions were distributed as powders. She could already feel the particles clinging to the insides of her nose and throat. Could already feel her head buzzing as the mixture began to work.

She commanded her feet to move. To run. But nothing was working right. The buzzing in her head was too loud now. Too loud to even hear the commands she was desperately trying to give her body.

Darkness encroached on the edges of her vision. She lost her hold on the bike, the chrome handlebars, now slick with the sweat from her palms, slipping out of her hands. She only dimly registered its crash to the pavement as she started to fall.

Strong hands grasped her arm. And then there was nothing.

TWENTY-EIGHT

There were flashes of consciousness through the darkness.

Pain in her head as she was shoved into a car.

The smell of leather.

A voice talking to someone a few feet away.

Then nothing. Again.

And finally, all at once, she was aware.

She tried to open her eyes. At first, her brain wouldn't listen. She struggled against the sensation that her eyelids were actually glued shut, the panic that she would never be able to open them again.

Finally, she opened them a crack, then a little more.

The room around her was familiar. Not home. Not Xander's or Sasha's. But a place she'd been before. She figured it out as soon as her eyes came to a stop on the pictures tacked to the wall.

Allegra was there. And Laura and Daniel and the Valcour twins and Xander and Sasha.

All of them with *X*s through their image.

She was in the house on Dauphine.

Her mind shrieked escape, but when she tried to sit up, an ice pick seemed to pierce her brain and she laid her head back, whimpering.

When the pain subsided, she realized that her hands were tied to the bedposts.

Panic bubbled up in her throat. She had no idea if anyone had seen her being taken or if they even knew she was missing. Did the man who knocked her out with the powder take her bike? Or did he leave it on the sidewalk where Xander would see it and know something was wrong?

If they had taken her bike, how long would it take Xander and Sasha to know she'd been kidnapped—that she hadn't just misunderstood their plan and started for home?

The questions came to an abrupt stop when she became aware of voices somewhere in the house. They were a vibration more than a sound, though she was dimly aware that one of them was higher in pitch than the others.

Breathe, Claire commanded her body, forcing her mind to stop running in circles.

And then: *Think.* There has to be a way out of this.

There has to be.

She took a few more deep breaths and looked around the room again, this time trying to locate any means of escape. She started with the bedside tables. If there was something sharp enough, maybe she could use her legs to get it to the bed, find a way to free herself from the rope that bound her wrists.

But they were bare. Not even a lamp stood on their surface.

She scanned the space beyond the bed. If she couldn't free herself, maybe she could find a way to escape once they tried to move her. They probably wouldn't keep her on the bed forever, and if they'd wanted to kill her outright, they would have done it already.

There was Eugenia's luggage, still against the wall. The bureau, an assortment of cosmetics and perfume bottles barely visible from Claire's position on the bed. A big mirror in the corner almost identical to one her mother had.

Could she break it? Use the pieces to fight her way out?

Maybe, but it would be messy and noisy. A last resort.

She came to the writing table and had to force her gaze away from the pictures on the wall. They brought forth a fresh batch of panic that served no purpose except to shut down her brain, make her unable to think straight.

She turned her attention back to the writing table, this time to its surface. A computer cord wound its way up from the floor, but the laptop it belonged to wasn't there. There was a stack of paper, and on top of it, an assortment of oddly shaped objects she couldn't quite decipher.

She lifted her head as much as she could with her hands tied to the bedpost, commanding her eyes to focus.

When everything finally came into view, she knew exactly what she was seeing. It was what they had expected. What the Cold Blood spell called for.

The forms were crude, but then appearance wasn't the point. Claire could make out the base of the shape, a T formed by two sticks with Spanish moss wound around them for shape. Claire was willing to bet each one had hair from the Guild's firstborns wound together with the moss.

Each doll was covered in different scraps of cloth—probably articles of clothing taken with the hair during the break-ins. The faces were nondescript, with black buttons for eyes and thread sewn in tiny x's where the mouths should be. The effect was twisted, a warped version of a child's toy.

The sight of them, on the desk and under the wall of photos, paralyzed her. For a minute, she couldn't do anything. Couldn't think about fighting or escape or anything at all.

All she could see was the dolls, their faces terrifying in their childish simplicity.

The murmuring in the hall was louder now and coming toward her. A second later, the door flung open and Eugenia marched into the room without so much as a glance at Claire.

As with the other times Claire had seen her, Eugenia was impeccably dressed, this time in a black cotton dress and simple sandals. Her hair was pulled back from her face, accentuating the harsh angles of her bone structure, the slight upturn of her eyes.

The man who'd doused Claire with the sedative powder entered the room on Eugenia's heels, glancing at Claire.

She tugged on the restraints.

"There's no point trying to get away," Eugenia said, her words harsh and clipped. She bent to check the ropes around Claire's wrists. "You won't be here long anyway."

What did she mean? Were they going to kill her?

"They're going to stop you," Claire said, desperate to delay whatever was coming, if only to give Xander and the others more time to find her. "They have everything they need now."

Eugenia advanced on the bed. Her eyes were cold and empty, devoid of emotion. She leaned closer, her perfume turning Claire's stomach.

"You understand very little. I almost feel sorry for you." She straightened, turning her eyes to the man. "Put her to sleep, Jean-Philip. Then gather everything together and bring it to the front hall."

Claire's mind grasped at Eugenia's words. They were going to move her. And once they left the house, Xander wouldn't have any idea where to start looking for her.

"Where are we going?" Claire asked, instinctively tugging on the ropes that bound her wrists. "Where are you taking me?"

"Quiet," Eugenia snapped. She turned to Jean-Philip. "Do it."

She left the room without a backward glance.

Claire turned her eyes on Jean-Philip as he moved across the room, lifting something from the top of the bureau.

"You don't have to do this. Please don't do this," she begged.

He came toward her, his hands cupped around something Claire couldn't see.

"Yes, I do," he said.

Then he opened his palm and blew, the gray powder dusting her face like snow.

She tried not to breathe it in, but it was a futile struggle. A second later she inhaled deeply, and the powder's fine particles made their way into her body.

She welcomed the darkness again.

TWENTY-NINE

Claire woke up as they were dragging her through the courtyard.

Jean-Philip had ahold of one of her arms. The other one was held too tightly by a smaller man with an iron grip.

She guessed this was Herve.

Claire's hands were tied behind her back, wrenching her shoulders into an awkward position that threw her off balance and made it hard to walk, even with the men on either side of her.

They hurried her toward the black Range Rover parked at the curb, both of them looking around as they left the courtyard to make sure they weren't seen.

She wondered how long it had been since she'd been standing in front of Sasha's with her bike. The sky was a deep blue, dark but illuminated by light in the distance. The temperature was no help. It was as hot and humid as it had been when she'd ridden her bike to Sasha's, the darkness offering no relief from the punishing heat.

She could hear the hum of the car's engine as they approached the Range Rover. Herve opened the back door, shoving her inside while Jean-Philip got in front.

Eugenia looked back at them from the driver's seat before she turned around, putting the car into gear and easing out into the street. The locks engaged on the doors with an ominous *thunk*.

Claire tried to pay attention to where they were going, but after a while she realized that it probably didn't matter. Wherever they were taking her, they didn't seem concerned that she could see the route, which meant they probably weren't expecting her to be around to tell anyone when all was said and done.

Eugenia didn't speak as she turned onto the highway, and Claire watched in silence as they headed out of town, north on Interstate 10. At first, she tried to keep her mind busy by analyzing possible escape routes, but it didn't take long to realize that her options were limited.

Unless they stopped the car en route to their destination, her only choice would be to make a break for the door on the off chance that she could unlock it and jump free while they sped through the darkness at seventy-five miles an hour.

Not exactly appealing.

She tried to calm herself by turning her head to the window, watching the broken-down houses and grim strip malls as they made their way farther out of town.

They passed a sign for Head of Island. Claire had a flash of Xander, sitting next to her in the Mercedes after they'd broken into the house on Dauphine, telling her he'd seen a map on the kitchen table. Now it all made sense.

Claire felt as far away from home as she'd ever been, even though they were probably only sixty miles or so outside of the city where she'd lived her whole life.

They drove without seeing another car in either direction, long stretches of forest broken only by an occasional trailer house or swampy lake.

After a few more miles, Eugenia pulled over to the side of the road. Claire sat up straighter, looking around and wondering if this was their intended destination. If it was, there wasn't much in the way of landmarks. Just miles of trees on either side of the road and a small house up ahead that looked so run-down Claire wondered if it was even habitable.

She got her answer when Eugenia turned to Jean-Philip, next to her in the front seat.

"I'm going to call Max. Let him know we're close."

She got out and stepped around the car to the shoulder of the road. Pulling a cell phone from the pocket of her tailored jacket, she turned away from them as she put the phone to her ear. A minute later, she walked over to the car and tapped on the window near Claire.

Herve leaned over, looking at Eugenia through the glass. She gestured for him to come, and he got out of the car, joining her by the side of the road as she talked on the phone.

Claire looked around. This was her chance. Possibly the one and only chance she would have to escape.

Herve was gone, his mouth moving as he said something to Eugenia, still on the phone. Claire hadn't heard the locks re-engage since he left, which meant the door was probably still unlocked. Jean-Philip was in the front seat, gazing out at Eugenia and Herve like that would help him hear what was being said between them and whoever was on the other end of Eugenia's phone.

Claire didn't know where she'd go once she was free. From the looks of things, she didn't have a lot of options. But she could make a run for it, maybe hide in the woods until they gave up on her.

Moving around without being obvious was hard to do, especially with her hands tied behind her back. In such close quarters, every sound she made seemed magnified—her bare legs sticking to the leather seats as she tried to move, the faint squeak of springs hidden in the seat of the car, the rustle of her hair against her shoulders. It all seemed so obviously loud that she was half surprised to find Jean-Philip still facing forward when she finally had her hands lined up with the door handle.

She took one last look at Eugenia, still standing at the side of the road with her phone to her ear. She gestured with one hand, her dress billowing against her legs in the summer breeze. Herve studied her with concentration, trying to follow the conversation while only hearing one side of it.

It was now or never.

Claire moved as close to the door as she could, feeling around for the handle. Her fingers brushed against hard plastic, then cool leather, and finally, smooth chrome.

She pulled, almost falling to the ground as the door opened behind her.

Everything happened all at once. The brief stumble as Claire tried to right herself, already moving around the back of the car to the road. The look of shock on Eugenia's face when she turned toward the noise and saw Claire moving away from them.

Then Claire didn't have time to continue looking. She ran as fast as she could, her restrained hands making it difficult to stay upright as she moved toward the street.

She heard Eugenia's voice behind her, barking, then yelling. But she didn't have time to decipher the words.

She looked right and left as she crossed the street, hoping to see someone—anyone—coming from either direction.

There was no one, and she was forced to continue across the pavement, throwing herself into the forest on the opposite side of the street. She half slid down the muddy embankment, trying to keep her balance as vines and branches tore at her bare legs. There was a fleeting thought of snakes. Of alligators and spiders and other things that could be lurking in the wild ferns and shrubs growing low to the ground.

But it didn't matter. She was more afraid of Eugenia—of Maximilian and what they planned to do to her—than she was of any creature in the swampland. She kept going, throwing herself into the forested gloom.

The darkness was her enemy and her friend. It made it difficult to see, difficult to avoid the low-hanging branches that smacked at her face, the vines that reached out like greedy hands to grab her legs.

She could only hope it made seeing her as difficult for Eugenia and the men.

She tripped and was compelled to look back even though she knew it would slow her down. It did her no good. She couldn't see a thing. She could only hear the rush of footsteps somewhere behind her, the patter of shoes against fallen leaves, an occasional shout as one of her pursuers called out to the others.

Finally, her lungs burning, she looked for a place to hide. She didn't know how much stamina Eugenia, Jean-Philip, and Herve had, but it was probably more than she had, with her arms tied and her brain still muddled. The rope on her wrists felt looser than it had before. Maybe if she stopped running she could free her hands.

She spotted a possibility in a large oak, its branches stretching toward the night sky. The tree itself offered minimal coverage, but there were a few large, moss-covered rocks near its base.

Her legs were tired, her breath coming in ragged gasps as she stepped over the wildflower bush growing around it. The biggest rock stood about two feet from the base of the tree. Claire dropped to the ground, resting her back against the tree's massive trunk and lowering her head below the top of the rock. From her vantage point, all she could see was the flowering bush that surrounded her. She would have to hope the same was true from the other side.

She couldn't hear Eugenia and the others. She used the time to test the confines of the rope around her wrists, wondering if it had been her imagination that it wasn't as tight.

But no. The rope *was* looser. She wriggled her hands back and forth, feeling the rope give a little more with each movement. A couple minutes later it dropped off her hands. She almost shouted with relief as she rubbed her wrists where the rope had cut into her skin.

Finally free, she attempted to quiet her raspy breathing as she listened for the sound of her pursuers in the distance. She was shaking, her teeth almost rattling, from fear. If her breathing didn't give her away, her chattering teeth just might.

Stop it, she ordered herself. *If you want to get out of this alive, you have to pull yourself together.*

A few seconds later, she heard them coming, their

footsteps rustling through the undergrowth. Their approach seemed to grow more careful as they neared, and Claire froze, wondering if she'd left some kind of evidence that she was in the vicinity, if they could somehow see her behind the rock.

Someone crashed through the trees to her right, stopping a few feet in front of the oak tree, close enough that Claire could hear the person breathing. She peered through the bushes, catching sight of a pair of athletic shoes. Had to be Jean-Philip or Herve. Eugenia was wearing sandals.

She let her eyes roam the ground without turning her head, afraid to make even the slightest sound. With one of her pursuers standing in front of her, she needed to get a lock on the other two. If she was spotted, she would have to make a run for it, and she didn't want to crash into them on her way out.

Finally, she caught sight of Eugenia, standing in a patch of moonlight to the left of the person she now realized was Jean-Philip. Both were very still, their heads tipped, eyes alert as if they sensed her nearby.

Two down, one to go.

Claire swept her gaze across the area in front of her. Where was Herve? Had he stayed at the car? Or was he lurking somewhere nearby?

She wondered if he was behind her, if maybe he was watching her at that very minute. She tried to resist the urge to look, but the longer she sat, Eugenia and Jean-Philip still only feet away, the more convinced she became that there was someone watching her.

When she couldn't stand it a second more, she turned her head, shifting slightly to see behind her. A twig snapped under her body. She froze, hoping it hadn't been as loud as it had seemed. But when she swiveled her head back around, Eugenia was already moving forward, her eyes locked on Claire's, even through the darkness.

Claire rose to a standing position, stumbling over the rock as she moved away from the tree. She looked back. Eugenia and Jean-Philip were only steps away.

Pushing herself up off the ground, she moved around the tree and made a run for it. She could still get away. Still find another hiding place.

She only got a few steps when she came up against something hard and unmoving.

A vise-like grip came down around her left arm. She only had a minute to look into Herve's eyes, devoid of any emotion, before something came down over head.

THIRTY

She didn't know what covered her face. It might have been a jacket or a bag. Whatever it was, it blocked out any and all light.

No one said a word after Herve grabbed her. He held her arm tightly, forcing her to move through the forest quickly, the darkness disorienting and terrifying. She stumbled and fell more than once. Each time, Herve yanked her to her feet, hauling her through the forest like she was nothing but a rag doll.

She smelled the road before they came to it. Hot asphalt and motor oil.

Then they were climbing up the embankment she had slid down when she'd made her escape. She knew they'd reached the top when her bare feet came down not on dirt and twigs and leaves but on the warm smooth surface of road.

Tears stung the backs of her eyelids as her terror grew. She wanted her mother with her sure voice and soft hands. Her father with his easy smile. Xander, who would never let anything bad happen to her if it was within his power to stop it. Sasha and even Allegra, who made her realize she wasn't as alone as she'd once thought.

They were almost back to the car. Once they had her inside, the doors locked, she was as good as dead.

A car door opened, and a second later she was shoved carelessly forward, her face and knees hitting the leather seat before she was able to right herself. She caught a whiff of familiar cologne as Herve scooted in next to her, his grip tight on her arm.

The car doors shut, and the engine roared to life. There was a moment of silence before Eugenia's voice drifted through the blackness.

"That was stupid." Her voice was terrifyingly calm. "We could have made it less painful for you, you know."

The car lurched forward.

✶

Claire lost all sense of time while they drove. Herve's hand remained around her arm, the covering still on her head. She was dimly aware that it was some kind of psychological ploy to head off another attempt at escape.

Keeping her disoriented and in the dark made her more complacent.

After a while—it could have been minutes or an hour—the car began to slow. Claire heard it in the engine, a subtle easing off of the gas.

They seemed to veer to the left, and the car left the asphalt, the tires crunching over gravel or rocky dirt. The ground was bumpy. Claire had to use her free hand to keep her body from hitting the door or ceiling of the car.

She was starting to feel motion sick when the car slowed to a stop. The engine was turned off and a second later, Eugenia spoke.

"Take off the hood."

It was instinct to shrink away from the hands that grazed her shoulders, despite the fact that she wanted to be able to see. The covering on her face was ripped off with a harsh tug.

Claire blinked, looking around rapidly, trying to get her bearings.

Eugenia was staring at her from the front seat, Herve still beside her in the back. She could see the back of

Jean-Philip's head in the front passenger seat. He didn't bother turning around.

Claire pressed herself against the door, wanting to be as far away from them all as she could.

"Let's go," Eugenia said. "Maximilian's already at the site."

Herve pulled on her arm, and this time, Claire fought. Every survival instinct she had told her that she couldn't let them take her into the dark, forested swamp where she could easily disappear.

She held on to the door handle, kicking Herve as he tried to yank her from the car.

He cursed, trying to keep ahold of her arm. Finally he reached toward her, landing a harsh smack across her face. It stung, but it was the shock of it that quieted her. She'd never been struck in her life. Ever. The smack was just more proof that her world had quickly changed. She was still reeling from it as Herve hauled her from the car.

Eugenia stepped angrily toward her. "We can put the hood back on," she hissed. "Is that what you want?"

Claire cringed, shaking her head. As terrifying as it was to be taken forcibly to the forest, it would be that much worse if she were plunged back into the utter blackness beneath the hood.

Eugenia stood up straighter, her eyes flashing. "Then behave yourself."

Jean-Philip moved to the back of the car and opened the hatch. Pulling three bags from it, he tossed one to Eugenia and shut the door. He slung the other two over one shoulder.

They started walking, Herve dragging Claire along.

She looked around, trying to get a handle on where they were. There wasn't much to go on. The Range Rover was parked in a small clearing, trees rising toward the sky on every side. There was a rusted iron bridge extending over a creek. A crooked, weathered sign was nailed to the tree, announcing the barely moving body of water as LOMAN'S CREEK. She hardly had time to register its name as they stepped onto the bridge and crossed over the water.

Then they were in the woods. Eugenia led the way, her steps confident. Herve and Claire walked behind her with Jean-Philip at the back of the line. Claire had no idea how Eugenia knew where they were going. Besides the bridge, there wasn't a single identifying characteristic as they moved through the trees and bushes of the forest.

The ground was soft and muddy. Every time Claire took a step, she sunk a little into the muck. She tried not to think about all the things that were down there, touching her bare feet every time she took a step. She was sure snakes were slithering around her ankles.

After what seemed like forever, Eugenia stopped. She turned in a circle, gazing at the trees like she saw something in them the rest of them couldn't, and continued to the left.

A couple minutes later, they stepped into a clearing. A wooden shack stood across an open meadow near the tree line on the other side. They were still a few feet from the structure when the door opened.

Maximilian stepped onto the slightly sunken porch, his face ghostly in the light of the partially full moon. Claire stopped moving, the suddenness of it forcing Herve to a stop, too.

Maximilian leaned against one of the posts that held up the roof, surveying her with eyes that seemed black in the darkness of night. Claire felt his ominous energy from across the clearing.

He turned around without a word, returning to the shack.

Herve forced Claire to move as Eugenia stepped onto the porch. They followed her inside, and Jean-Philip shut the door behind them.

They were in a main room, a fire crackling in what looked to be a makeshift fireplace against one wall. Claire wondered why anyone would want to light a fire in Louisiana during the month of July. It was hotter inside the shack than it had been outside. Sweat trickled down her back.

The room was sparsely furnished with a torn sofa, mismatched chairs, and a cracked wooden table that sat on the far side of the room. A doorway stood to the right of a tiny refrigerator.

Herve crossed the room with Claire in tow, shoving her down onto one of the chairs like he was glad to finally be rid of her. But he didn't leave her side.

Eugenia and Maximilian disappeared through the doorway into the other room. The walls were thin. Claire could hear murmuring, but she couldn't make out what they were saying. She looked around the room, hoping for some chance of escape, a weapon, anything.

There was nothing.

Maximilian stepped from the room with Eugenia on his heels. He walked past Claire, and a wave of bleakness washed over her.

"Outside," he said, the same exotic accent in his voice

Claire remembered from his conversation with Estelle behind the carriage house.

The word must have been meant for Jean-Philip and Herve. They followed Maximilian to the front door without a word.

Eugenia came toward Claire, grabbing her by the arm. "Get up."

Claire obeyed. She didn't have much of a choice and her arm was already bruised where Herve had used it to drag her through the forest.

She felt a moment's hope when Eugenia led her to the doorway. It was just the two of them now. Maybe there would be a better chance of escape in the other room.

Eugenia shoved her through the doorway and into a tiny room lit by a single candle. Claire glanced around, looking for anything she could use to her advantage. Her hopes were quickly dashed. The room was probably intended as a place to sleep, but it was just as bare as the other one. Worse, this one didn't have a single window, and its only furnishings were a wooden desk and a chair that matched those in the living room.

"There's a rag and some water inside the basin," Eugenia said, tipping her head at a metal tub on top of the desk. "Use it to wash yourself for the ceremony and then put on the ritual garment."

Claire shook her head. "I'm not changing. Whatever you're going to do to me, you'll have to do it in these clothes."

Eugenia hands were lightning fast as she reached toward Claire, holding her with one arm while she began tugging at her tank top with the other.

"Wait! What are you *doing?*" Claire shouted.

"You'll wash and change for the ceremony as instructed. It's a matter of respect for the loas. And if you don't, I'll change you myself."

Claire shrunk back, crossing her arms over her chest. "Fine! I'll do it. Just . . . leave me alone for a minute."

Eugenia considered the request, an internal struggle visible on her face. Finally she nodded. "If you give me any more trouble, I'll get Max. Let him deal with you. Do you understand?"

The thought of being in close proximity to Max again was enough to turn Claire complacent. "Yes."

Eugenia was almost out the door when Claire called out to her, unable to keep silent the question that had been burning in her mind since she'd woken up at the house on Dauphine.

"Why are you doing this?" she asked, her voice trembling as she tried not to cry. "I know about Max . . . Maximilian. About Elisabeta. But why you?"

Eugenia seemed to flinch with the mention of Elisabeta, and for one brief second, her face seemed to crumple. Then she composed herself, standing straighter.

"Did you think Elisabeta was born without a mother?" She closed the door behind her.

Claire dropped onto the chair, her breath coming shallow and fast. Maximilian and Eugenia were Elisabeta's parents.

Now Claire knew they would never let her go.

THIRTY-ONE

Eugenia came into the room just after Claire washed and dressed in the white garment, leaving her own clothes on the floor near the chair.

"Come with me," she said.

Claire walked toward the door.

Eugenia didn't move. She just stood there, blocking the doorway, staring at Claire with a strange expression on her face. She flinched when Eugenia reached out to straighten the garment, moving Claire's long hair back from her shoulders.

"I hope you understand that my motives are different from Max's," she said softly.

Stunned by the change in Eugenia's demeanor, Claire didn't speak.

"Max wants revenge," Eugenia continued. "And, while I don't blame him, it's my intent to restore balance to the equation. A life was needlessly taken. My daughter's life. It's only right that someone be held accountable for the crime. That your power is so strong is your misfortune."

Claire shook her head. "But it's not. I don't even believe. I've never believed."

Eugenia smiled, an eerie, knowing light in her eyes.

She reached for Claire's hand. "Come."

Claire wondered if the others were waiting, but the main room was empty. Eugenia led her through it to the front door.

The first thing that caught Claire's eye when they stepped onto the porch was the fire. It had been lit in the center of the clearing, and while it wasn't huge, it was obviously meant to be the center of the ritual.

Claire wasn't surprised to see black candles lit in a ring around it, but it still brought forward a new surge of panic. Colored candles were used for all kinds of spellcraft and ritual, the colors corresponding to different kinds of work.

Black candles were the most dangerous of all, used to summon the darkest forces of the spiritual world, something that was risky even when done by an experienced priest or priestess.

Maximilian was sitting cross-legged on one side of the fire, Herve and Jean-Philip in the same position across from him. She could see the resemblance between them in the light of the fire; the same angular features, the same dark eyes. A wooden platform, too low to the ground to be a table, stood very near the flames.

Claire stopped walking. She knew a sacrificial altar when she saw one.

She held on to the door frame as Eugenia stepped forward.

When she realized Claire wasn't with her she looked back. "Come, now."

Claire shook her head as she frantically eyed the field.

Eugenia turned toward the men. "Herve. Jean-Philip."

They stood, and Claire saw that they, too, were in white tunics. They came toward her, stepping onto the porch and grabbing her arms. They carried her down the steps like she weighed nothing at all, even though she kicked and screamed every step of the way.

She tried to dig her feet into the wild grass and mud as they hauled her across the field, but it did no good. Herve and Jean-Philip just raised her higher, her feet too far off the ground to be of any help.

Maximilian remained seated as they approached.

Claire was only dimly aware that she was still scream-
ing. That it was her voice echoing across the clearing,
although the words were unintelligible.

It didn't matter. There was no one to hear her.

Herve and Jean-Philip lifted her onto the altar, laying
her on her back. She tried to sit up, to struggle against
them, but they were stronger than they looked. Herve
held her down while Jean-Philip tied her wrists and ankles to the legs of the altar.

She flailed and thrashed, testing the strength of the
bonds. They held fast.

Now Maximilian rose. He moved around the fire,
murmuring to each of the others. Herve sat back on the
ground, a drum between his legs. Eugenia pulled something from the pocket of her tunic, bringing it over to
Jean-Philip, who was mixing something in a basin on the
ground.

They seemed oblivious to her, like she wasn't tied up
right in front of their eyes.

Herve began to beat on the drum, and the atmosphere changed instantly. Claire recognized the subtle
shift, had felt it before in rituals and ceremonies, though
if someone had asked her about it prior to tonight she
wouldn't have been able to put her finger on it. The beat

was primal. It moved through the air as Herve began to chant in French.

Jean-Philip moved with the rhythm of the drum, his face transformed. He was no longer the staid mannequin Claire had seen uptown, but a voodoo priest lost in the beat of the rite.

Eugenia and Maximilian turned their backs on the fire and bent to the ground, picking something up. Claire saw what it was a moment later when they each lifted elaborate feathered headdresses onto their heads.

They would act as the high priest and priestess in the ritual, Houngan and Mambo, summoning the loas. Claire wondered which of them would give their blood for the spell that would turn the blood of the firstborns cold.

She hardly recognized them as they turned back to the fire. It was more than the ritual garb. It was something in their eyes. A far-off gaze that made Claire think they weren't there in the field at all but somewhere else completely.

Eugenia started to move, too, bending and jumping and prostrating around the fire in time to the beat, moving in opposition to Jean-Philip's position. The chic European woman Claire had met in the store that first day was gone, replaced by a Mambo queen whose connection to the ancient, primal craft was evident in every movement.

Claire thought Maximilian would join in. Instead, he bent again to the grass. When he rose and came toward her, she saw the shine of a knife blade in his hand.

She was momentarily shocked into stillness as her brain processed what was happening. He was coming toward her, a knife in one hand, small bowls in the other.

She heard Xander's voice on that faraway afternoon outside the house on Dauphine.

They bled you . . .

And then, in the car on the way to Eddie's as he told her about his dream: *I can't get to you, Claire.*

It hadn't been a dream after all. It had been a prophecy. They were going to use her blood to fulfill Marie's addendum. Maximilian was going to bleed her, and Xander wouldn't be able to save her.

He'd already seen it.

She started to thrash again as Maximilian came closer. "No. . . . No! You have it wrong. I'm not the one. I don't even believe." Claire was crying now, desperate. "I'm sorry about Elisabeta, but it wasn't my fault. It wasn't *our* fault. We were just kids."

He bent down when he reached her side. She couldn't see what he was doing, but when he stood, he didn't have the bowls. She guessed he'd placed them under her somewhere to collect the blood.

His face was so close to hers that she could see his eyes, but there was no pity there. Only concentration as he lifted her right arm and lowered the knife blade to the tender skin of her forearm.

She turned her head away, trying to lose herself in the rhythm of the drumbeat, the otherworldly chanting coming from Eugenia and Jean-Philip. A second later she felt the knife bite into her skin followed by a warm trickle onto her wrist, hand, fingertips.

Maximilian moved to the other side of her body, repeating the motion with her other arm.

Then he was walking away, joining the dance around the fire, his own voice rising to meet the voices of the others.

Claire's head began to feel fuzzy. The events around her became increasingly surreal, like it wasn't her on the altar at all, but someone else. Someone whose eyes were barely open, whose blood ran like a river down her arms, pooling in the bowls underneath them.

After that there were only flashes of consciousness as her hold on reality slowly slipped away.

The flicker of the fire casting strange shadows on Jean-Philip's face as he danced.

Darkness.

Maximilian dipping something into the bowls he'd placed on the ground, using it to paint a circle around the ritual site. Was the circle painted in her blood? She couldn't be sure.

Darkness.

Max, lifting one of the bowls underneath her hand, pouring a thick, dark liquid into the basin of ingredients that Jean-Philip had been mixing when they first tied her to the altar.

Darkness.

And then Eugenia, pulling the dolls from her pockets. The dolls with hair and clothes from Xander and Sasha and Allegra and the rest of the Guild's firstborns.

She submersed the first one in the mixture, lifting it into the air, liquid dripping from it as she howled her requests to the loas.

She set it beside the black candles and moved on to the next one.

Claire tried to stay alert, but she couldn't help the slip

into unconsciousness. When she came to, she had no idea how many of the doll babies Eugenia had already done or how many were left.

Was she wrong? Was her blood powerful enough to use in the Cold Blood spell? Were Xander and Sasha already dying? Was it quick? Painful?

I don't believe, Claire reminded herself, moving her head back and forth in a gesture of denial.

She muttered the words. "I don't believe . . . I don't believe . . ."

She knew no one could hear her over the chanting and the beat of the drum, but she said it anyway.

Eugenia was poised over the basin with another doll baby, preparing to lower it into the mixture, when she suddenly stopped.

She looked up, her gaze drifting to the forest surrounding the clearing, her body still, even as Maximilian and Jean-Philip continued the ritual, Herve still drumming.

Then Max's movements slowed, his gaze following Eugenia's.

Claire tried to lift her head. Tried to see what they saw.

But when she finally focused on the figures moving toward the fire, her mind couldn't make sense of it.

At first, she only saw two. Two people moving toward them from the forest.

Then there were more. Three, four, five . . . Claire wasn't sure how many.

The drumbeat slowed and then stopped altogether as the figures came closer.

THIRTY-TWO

Claire turned her head, willing her eyes to focus on what she was seeing. Who she was seeing.

Then, like a dream, she heard Xander's voice.

"You didn't think you're the only ones who can work spells, did you?"

Everything went quiet and still. Herve stopped drumming, his face a mask of shock. Eugenia, Maximilian, and Jean-Philip were rooted in place, their eyes focused on the approaching figures.

Xander was moving swiftly toward her, fury in his eyes like Claire had never seen. And he wasn't alone. Sasha was moving across the clearing, too. And Allegra and Laura and Charlie and William Valcour.

The Guild's firstborns.

The only one missing was little Daniel.

And then, like a specter, Eddie appeared in the clearing,

the strong planes of his face pulled into an expression of calm determination. He wasn't wearing a headpiece, although he did have on a ceremonial tunic, but in the light of the fire, he looked every bit as imposing as Maximilian.

They had all emerged from the forest at the same time, but from different places. Now they advanced on the fire, on Maximilian and Eugenia and the others, in a circular pattern, closing in on them from all sides.

Xander had almost reached Claire's side when Maximilian seemed to shake loose from his shock.

"I wouldn't come any closer," he said, his voice a warning. "We've started the ritual. Three of you are already marked for death. The question is . . . which three?"

Xander didn't even slow down. "And all of you are marked by us. The question is . . . for what?"

He reached Claire's side. There was so much love and pain in his eyes that she tried to reach up and touch his face. But her arms wouldn't move, both because of the restraints and the blood loss that made her so weak she just wanted to sleep and sleep.

"I'm going to get you out of here," he said softly.

She thought it might hurt when he untied the ropes on her wrists, but she didn't feel a thing.

He lifted her into his arms. She tried to protest, to tell

him she could walk on her own. But she couldn't seem to formulate the words. She was so overcome with relief at the feel of his arms around her, his breath in her hair, that all she could do was wrap her bleeding arms around his neck and hold on.

Eugenia, taller and more imposing in her headpiece, turned on him. "You have a long way to go before your power is equal to ours, boy."

"Alone, that might be true," Xander said, turning to leave with Claire in his arms. "But I'm not alone."

He turned away from the fire, removing Claire from the ritual circle as Eddie, Sasha, Allegra, and the others stepped forward.

Claire wanted to call out to them, to tell them Maximilian and Eugenia were dangerous. But the firstborns weren't retreating.

They were advancing.

And Eddie was leading the way.

They held up dolls to the firelight as they began to chant in unison. Understanding threaded its way into Claire's mind; Xander had taken things from the house on Dauphine. Personal things.

And the firstborns—along with Eddie—had used them to make dolls of their own.

They spoke in French as they moved forward. Claire shouldn't have been able to understand, but inexplicably, she did. She heard their call to the loa Bosou Koblamin, defeater of enemies. Understood their request for intervention, their demand for the evil ones to cease their use of dark power in the name of vengeance. A call for the return to balance that existed when the spirits were summoned in the name of goodness, health, and love.

The drumming started up again, a perfect rhythm to the words of the ritual, but when Claire looked over Xander's shoulder at Herve, he was standing near the fire with the others as the firstborns closed in around them, forcing them inside a ritual circle of their own making.

His hands weren't moving over the drum.

The drumbeat was coming from inside her. It *was* her. And suddenly the words were right there. She knew what they meant, knew what to say. She murmured the words as Xander took her toward the forest, adding her voice, however small, to the others as they chanted.

She and Xander were almost to the tree line when she saw Allegra break free of the circle. She ran toward them as a loud *whoosh* erupted from the ritual circle. Claire watched over Xander's shoulder, transfixed as smoke swirled around the fire, rising in a column from its center. Then it wasn't a column but a serpent, rising into the air, undulating around the circle, lashing out with a forked tongue that seemed more dangerous than any snake in the bayou.

Not wanting to leave Sasha and the others behind to face whatever beast Maximilian and Eugenia had conjured, Claire cried out, "Wait! Xander, wait!"

He stopped jogging toward the forest and looked back as Allegra reached their side.

"It's okay," she said. "That isn't them. It's us."

"Us?"

"Yeah, us. The Guild. The firstborns." Allegra smiled. "With a little help."

"But we can't just leave them here," Claire said.

"Trust me," Allegra said. "As long as they're together, no one can stop them. And they need to keep Maximilian and the others busy. We have our own work to do."

"Work?" Claire repeated. Her teeth started to chatter despite the sweat that slicked her body and caused the tunic to stick to her skin. "What work?"

Xander looked at Allegra. "She's lost a lot of blood. We need to work fast."

"Let's hurry then." Allegra led the way into the forest.

The fire receded behind them as they stepped into the

trees. The drumbeat was still there, still inside Claire's mind, as they moved quickly through the woods.

"What are we doing?" she finally managed to mumble as she was jostled against Xander's shoulder. "Where are we going?"

"This is far enough," Xander said, stopping. "I need to slow the bleeding before we can do anything else."

He lowered Claire gently onto the forest floor, turning to look at Allegra over his shoulder. "Get everything ready. As soon as I have her arms bandaged, we need to move."

"I don't want to move anymore," Claire protested, shivering.

"Don't worry," he said gently. "We're almost done. I have to tear some pieces off this thing you're wearing, okay? It'll stop the bleeding better than my T-shirt."

She nodded.

He reached for the bottom of the tunic and tugged, ripping two strips off the garment almost before Claire knew what was happening. Lifting her right arm, he sucked in his breath when he saw the extent of her injuries.

"How bad is it?" Allegra said from somewhere behind Claire.

"They weren't fooling around, that's for sure." He

looked into Claire's eyes. "I'm going to be as careful as I can, Claire, okay?"

"Okay." She wasn't scared. She couldn't feel anything anyway, even when he began winding the first strip of fabric around her arm.

He knotted it, repeating the action with the strip on her other arm.

He looked up at Allegra. "Everything ready to go?"

She nodded, pulling something from a black backpack Claire hadn't noticed before. A second later, she heard the strike of a match and a small, orange flame bloomed in Allegra's fingers. She lit a row of gray and purple candles, setting them in a circle around Claire.

"What are we doing?" she asked them.

Xander lowered his face to hers. "We didn't get to you in time. Max had started the Cold Blood spell, and they'd already covered three of the dolls in the potion. The only reason three of us aren't dead is because we interrupted the ritual, but if they try to continue, it'll all come down to who's stronger. It's a close call with Eddie on our side, but we need to use Marie's counterspell to make sure everyone will be okay."

Claire shook her head. "I don't know how to use it. I don't know how to do anything."

"You know more than you think," Xander insisted.

"You're wrong," she said, looking away. "I don't even know if I believe."

Allegra knelt next to her in the dirt. "Look at me, Claire." Her voice was harsh. "You don't have to believe. You're the one. The one mentioned in Marie's counter-spell. 'One with enough power to summon the loas,' remember?"

"That's not me," Claire protested.

"Yes, it is. Don't you see? It's why they wanted you."

Claire tried to pull the counterspell from the haze of her memory. "Even if it were true, we don't have every-thing else."

Allegra pulled the black backpack up near Claire's body. "You dropped the book when they took you. We brought everything we need. Everything except you. Will you try?"

Claire's memory of the ceremony was fuzzy, but she knew Xander was right; Maximilian and Eugenia had already started the Cold Blood spell. She recalled the dolls, their submersion in the potion mixed with her blood, the liquid dripping from them in the light of the fire.

How long would it be before one of them stopped

breathing? Before their heart was unable to pump the thick, cold blood running through their veins?

"There wasn't a spell," she said. "In the book. There was only a recipe for the potion. I don't know what to say or do."

"It doesn't matter what you say or how you say it," Allegra insisted. "Remember? The power is yours to call on whenever you need it."

Claire hesitated one last time before nodding. "I'll try."

Relief washed over Allegra's face, and Claire realized for the first time that her friend was scared. Maybe she hadn't had her veins sliced open or been held up for sacrifice by Maximilian and Eugenia, but Allegra's risk was every bit as great as her own.

Xander held a hand out toward Allegra. "Give me the container."

Allegra placed a ceramic container in Xander's hand. He removed the lid and set it on the ground.

"I have to undo one of these bandages for a minute. Is that okay?"

Claire nodded.

He bent to kiss her forehead before unwinding the strip of fabric on her right arm. As soon as the pressure was off the wound, a fresh trickle of blood oozed down Claire's forearm. Xander held it over the open container, letting it drip for a minute before handing it back to Allegra.

He rewrapped Claire's bandage while Allegra mixed Claire's blood into the other ingredients.

"Okay," she said. "Ready."

"It'll be easier if you stand," Xander said to Claire. "Do you think you can manage it if we help you?"

"I think so."

Xander took one of her arms. Allegra took the other, and they helped her to her feet. Claire swayed, the forest tilting wildly as she tried to regain her balance.

"It's okay," Xander reassured her. "We've got you."

Her head cleared a little and she looked around, trying to find something—anything—she could fix her gaze on to keep everything from turning upside down again. It was dark, the trees in the forest a blur of shadow around her. She finally settled on the candles near her feet, focusing her eyes on their flickering flames.

"What do I do?"

"I'm going to sprinkle the potion around your feet," Allegra said. "I'll use a counterhex spell, but while I do that, you need to call on the spirits in your own way.

Just . . . I don't know. Call on the loas. On any spirit being who offers protection to those under threat."

Claire took a deep breath, feeling foolish for being self-conscious. There were more important things at stake than her pride. She had to try.

Allegra took the ceramic container, tipping it and sprinkling the potion near Claire's feet, around the candles on the ground. Allegra spoke in a murmur that gradually rose, the words coming slowly at first and then in a rush of French. Some of the powder blew across the flames, sending a hiss into the air around them.

When she had completed the circle with the potion, she tipped the rest of the container into her hands, offering up the rest of the mixture to the night sky as she continued to chant. Her face was beautiful and terrifying, her dark hair spilling down her back. The power she wielded was almost undeniable, even to Claire.

Then Xander's voice joined with Allegra's, speaking the same words.

Claire closed her eyes, needing to block out all the reminders of her real life.

A life with bicycles and yoga and college. A life of reason.

She spoke softly, the words a whisper, even to her own

ears. She started by asking, just asking for help, pleading with the loas and Marie and the others who had gone before her to intervene, to help her right the wrong that had been committed against the Guild firstborns.

The words came faster as something instinctual took over, the drumbeat resuming within her body, marking time to a spell she somehow knew. A spell that seemed to have lived in the shadows of her consciousness all this time, for ages and ages, for centuries and eons, waiting for the time when she would call upon it.

She only dimly registered that she was speaking in French, the words of the spell, a plea to the loas, coming as surely as if she'd memorized them from some long-ago spell book. She repeated them over and over, a presence building inside her that was both familiar and strange, both part of her and something entirely other.

The presence grew, demanding release as she continued to chant, filling her up until it seemed to overflow, pouring out of her hands and fingers, into the ground at her feet, escaping into the air that she breathed. It swooped around her, picking up smoke from the candles, winding its way around and around them like a tornado until they stood within a solid column of wind, the roar of it filling every crevice of Claire's body.

Without knowing how, she gathered it, commanded it, asked it to do her bidding. To counter Maximilian's spell and render him powerless against them. To cease whatever actions he might be continuing in the field in front of the shack.

The wind swirled faster, its agitation palpable as it took its cue from Claire. It rose into the sky, twisting and turning until it was a serpent identical to the one commanded by the firstborns as Xander had taken Claire into the forest. Claire watched as it propelled itself purposefully across the sky, heading toward the smoke rising from the other ritual site.

The air was quiet in the wake of the departing spirit. But Claire's skin was on fire, the surface of it tingling with pins and needles like her whole body had been asleep and had only just awoken.

When she opened her eyes, she was surprised to find that her arms were stretched toward the sky, her hands covered in a powdery, metallic residue that must have been the potion Allegra had mixed.

She wondered if the spirit had gotten to the others in time. If it had stopped Maximilian and Eugenia.

She looked at Xander and Allegra, still staring at the sky, but before she could say anything a drop of cool liquid hit her face. She tipped her head back as three more droplets hit her face.

A second later it was torrential. Rain streamed from the sky like a waterfall, drenching Claire's hair and the white tunic.

She let it wash her clean. Let it wash away her fear and doubt.

When her legs finally gave out beneath her, her body falling to the wet, loamy earth, there was only wonder.

THIRTY-THREE

This is what she remembered.

The rush through the forest, her body snug against Xander's, her head bumping against his shoulder.

The rain, still falling. Not a cold drizzle but a healing warmth, washing her clean.

Allegra's warm hand on Claire's forehead. Her voice: "She's too cold."

Sasha's eyes, dark and worried, when she spoke. "It's okay, Claire. Everything's okay. You did it."

Then, the feel of cool leather against the back of her legs, her head in Xander's lap. His head bowed over hers, tears falling onto her face.

She reached up to touch him, her blood-streaked hand resting against his cheek.

THIRTY-FOUR

Claire had been in bed nearly a week, hardly allowed out of her room to go to the bathroom. At first, she hadn't minded. She'd been so weak that she could hardly keep her eyes open, even after the blood transfusion she'd received at the hospital.

Finally, she'd woken up feeling different. Clearheaded and alert.

Throwing a sweater over her boxers and T-shirt, she left her room, pausing in the hallway as she wondered where her mother might be. A moment later, she headed for the ritual room.

She waited by the closed door, listening to her mother's soft murmuring from the other side. Finally, she turned the knob and let the door swing open slowly.

Her mother was there, dressed in the white tunic, her hair long and flowing over her shoulders. Somehow the tunic didn't inspire the fear Claire would have expected after Maximilian and Eugenia had forced her to wear it.

It was just a piece of fabric. There were stacks more like it in the store downstairs.

Even more surprising, the sight of her mother, eyes closed and kneeling in front of the candlelit altar, didn't scare her, either.

She tried to remember why her mother had seemed so frightening in ritual when Claire was a child. Now, she looked peaceful, her face beautiful as she murmured the words to a protection spell.

Claire wasn't surprised when she spoke without turning her head.

"Come in, Claire." She hesitated. "If you'd like."

Claire stepped into the room. The smell of anise hung in the air.

Anise and eucalyptus and lemongrass.

Claire inhaled deeply. Her shoulders relaxed as the scent worked its way into her body.

White candles were lined up in front of a picture of her, a powdery residue scattered across the surface of the table.

Claire turned away, scanning the room. She found what she was looking for on the mantel above the fireplace, and she made her way to it, lifting the framed photograph and carrying it back to the altar table.

She placed the picture of her mother and father, taken at some long-ago picnic, on the altar. Pilar watched as Claire reached for an unlit candle. Placing it in front of the picture of her parents, she struck a match and lit the wick, watching the flame spring to life.

She sank to the floor next to her mother, their lips moving in unison, calling on the loas to protect each other.

ـ໑ـ

Claire was rocking on the porch swing, trying to concentrate on a book, when Sasha came up the walkway.

"Wow, Sleeping Beauty's finally awake," she said.

Claire laughed, setting her book aside. "Very funny. I needed it."

Sasha stepped onto the porch, lowering herself next to Claire on the swing.

"Feeling better?"

"Much," Claire said. "Still tired, believe it or not. But at least now I can get through the morning without needing a nap."

Sasha nodded. "They said that you're lucky to be alive."

Claire swallowed hard. It was true. She remembered the first time she'd seen them change her bandages at the hospital, the long vertical cuts Max had made along the veins of her forearms.

Xander's words from the forest had drifted back to her: *They weren't fooling around.*

The cuts weren't meant to eke a little blood out of Claire for their ritual.

They were meant to bleed her dry.

She took a deep breath, trying to banish the fear that always crept over her when she thought about Maximilian and Eugenia. When she thought about how their love for little Elisabeta had twisted into something dark and ugly in the wake of their grief.

"They say I'm going to be okay," she said softly, reaching out to take Sasha's hand. "Thanks to you guys."

Sasha smiled. "We could say the same for you."

After Claire had gotten home from the hospital, it was Allegra who had told her about the doll babies that had already been immersed in the potion containing her blood.

One of them had been Allegra's. One of them had been Laura's.

And one had been Xander's.

They sat in silence for a few more minutes before Sasha spoke again. "How are your parents handling everything?"

Claire sighed. "I think they feel guilty. You know, that they weren't the ones to save us."

Allegra had told Claire the story. How Sasha and Xander had gone to their parents and told them everything after they found Claire's bike. How the Guild had called the police and reported Claire missing instead of asking Allegra or someone else in the Guild to help find her. How it had rocked the firstborns, seeing their parents turn to law enforcement instead of the craft when they were supposedly its biggest advocates.

It was the firstborns who'd taken matters into their own hands, calling on Eddie and using Allegra's second sight to see the sign for Loman's Creek and the bridge Claire had been marched across by Eugenia, Herve, and Jean-Philip.

"Any word on Maximilian?" Sasha asked her after a couple of minutes.

Claire shook her head. "And Eugenia and her sons still aren't talking."

Once they'd gotten away from the ritual site, one of the Valcour twins had contacted their parents with the license plate of the Range Rover. The police had picked all three of them up a few miles from the site.

Maximilian hadn't been with them.

"So he really got away." There was defeat in Sasha's voice.

Claire had to swallow the fear that rose in her at the thought of Maximilian roaming the streets.

"For now."

"Have you seen Xander?" Sasha asked.

"He's been by a couple of times, but I've been so out of it. I don't even remember what we talked about."

"He's been worried sick about you," Sasha said. "I don't even think he's bothered to hide it from his parents."

Claire thought about it, wondering how Estelle Toussaint felt about her only son loving a disbelieving voodoo heiress who had spent most of her life wanting nothing more than to escape the confines of their tradition.

Then she realized it didn't really matter.

✧

She was wheeling her bike out of the store when she ran into her dad, replacing the lid on one of the trash cans on the pathway that ran along the side of the house.

He eyed her bike dubiously. "You sure you're ready for that?"

Claire nodded. "I think so. I feel better. A lot better. And I need to get out. Get some fresh air. I've been cooped up in the house for almost two weeks. Besides, I want to see Xander."

He smacked his hands together to clean them off. "I'm not sure your mom's going to be too happy about your riding around town just yet."

Claire knew he was worried about Maximilian. That he was still out there somewhere.

"I can't stay home forever." She stepped forward, kissing her dad on the cheek. Then she reached into her shirt and pulled out the gris-gris bag that Xander had given her when they'd gone to see Eddie. She'd worn it inside her shirt ever since she'd come home from the hospital. "Besides, tell her I'm wearing this."

The worry didn't leave his eyes, but a slow smile crept across his mouth. "Be careful. And text me when you get to the Toussaints'."

She swung one leg over the bicycle seat. "Will do, Dad. See ya."

She pedaled down the driveway and into the street. Her legs were weak at first, like she was learning to ride a bike all over again. But as she came closer to the Garden District, the city's heavy, warm wind brushing her face like a friend, she started to feel free for the first time in ages.

The skin on her forearms was tight as she gripped the handlebars, the wounds under her bandages starting to itch as they healed. She would have scars forever. It was something she'd learn to live with.

Her stomach fluttered a little as she turned onto Xander's street. Even though he'd been to her house more than once over the past couple of weeks, this was the first time Claire really felt in control.

Like she knew what she wanted.

It was surprisingly scary. Knowing what you wanted also meant the possibility of losing it.

She'd learn to live with that, too.

She pulled through the gates at the head of the Toussaints' driveway, slowing when she came to the house. She walked the bike to the fence and leaned it against the iron railing.

"Claire!" Sophie came bounding from the side of the house, throwing herself at Claire. Her forearms stung as she wrapped her arms around Sophie's small body, but she didn't mind. It was the first time someone had treated her like they used to. Like she was still the same old Claire and not something fragile and broken.

"Is Xander home?" she asked.

Sophie nodded. "In the house. I'd take you, but I'm playing hide-and-seek with Betsy and I don't have much time left."

"I understand," Claire said with a smile. "I know the way in."

She skipped off, and Claire headed for the porch. She was almost to the stairs when Betsy opened the front door.

"Claire! My goodness, child! What are you doing here? Aren't you still recovering?"

Claire stopped at the bottom of the stairs, already a little tired. "I'm feeling a lot better, actually." She remembered Sophie. "I thought you were playing hide-and-seek with Sophie."

"Psh! I just tell her that to get her out from under my feet now and then," she said.

Claire laughed. "Nice! Um . . . Is Xander around?"

Betsy grinned, stepping onto the porch. "He sure is. And I'm willing to bet you'll wipe the sour look off his face, too. Been carrying it around ever since that night."

Claire wasn't sure how much Betsy knew, but the police had been told it was a garden-variety kidnapping by a voodoo nutcase. Since Eugenia, Herve, and Jean-

Philip weren't talking, it was doubtful they were going to say anything different.

"Let me help you now," Betsy said, starting down the steps. "Alexandre is in the—" She stopped as Xander came out onto the porch, followed by Estelle and Bernard, and surprisingly, Eddie Clement. "Oh, there he is!"

She'd come to see Xander, but she couldn't hide her surprise at seeing Eddie, standing on the Toussaints' porch like it was the most natural thing in the world.

"Eddie?"

He hurried down the steps with open arms, squeezing her in an embrace. The scent of sandalwood drifted to her from his printed tunic.

He pulled back, studying her face. "You look pretty good, all things considered."

"Thanks to you," she said. "You and everyone else."

He chuckled. "Are you kidding? I've wanted to lead a black magic smackdown for years." His expression darkened. "But I am glad you're okay. You had us worried there for a while."

She smiled. "What are you doing here?"

Eddie glanced back at the Toussaints. "Let's just say the Toussaints and I were discussing a potential partnership. But that's Guild business. I'll tell you all about it later." He looked at Xander. "I'm guessing you have more important things on your mind."

He headed down the walkway.

"We'll see you Tuesday," Bernard called out to him.

Tuesday? Claire felt like she'd woken up in some kind of alternative reality. That was the only way to explain the fact that the Toussaints were being friendly to Eddie Clement. That they were talking about Guild *business* with him.

Obviously, a lot had happened in the weeks she'd been recovering.

Claire turned to Xander. All of the fear and pain seeped out of her at the sight of him.

He stepped off the porch and then stopped. She saw the conflict in his eyes as his parents stood watching.

Claire looked at the Toussaints, not wanting to be rude. "Hello, Aunt Estelle and Uncle Bernard."

Bernard put his arm around his wife. "Hello, Claire. Are you feeling better?"

She nodded. "Much, thank you."

She moved toward Xander, her eyes on him every step of the way. She didn't stop until she was right in front of him, only a couple of inches between their bodies.

She looked up, feeling shy. "Hi."

He swallowed nervously. "Hi."

"I hope it's okay that I came," she said.

"It's more than okay," he said softly.

He stood still, his hands at his sides. Waiting, she knew, for her.

She took a step forward and stood on her tiptoes, wrapping her arms around his neck as Estelle and Bernard looked on.

She breathed in the smell of him, the feel of him. "I've missed you."

His arms snaked around her waist, pulling her tight against him. "I've missed you, too."

There were still things she didn't know.

She didn't know what she believed. If she had really saved the firstborns—and if they had really saved her. If she had really seen the loas rise into the night sky to protect them or if it had been a product of her imagination and the massive blood loss she'd endured. If she would grow into her place in the Guild or travel another path entirely.

But she knew that she wasn't alone. That there were people who loved her, who would come to her aid if she needed them. That she was part of something honored and true. Something worth holding on to.

Most of all, she knew that she loved Xander.

That she believed in him. In them.

And as he took her hand and turned to his parents with a smile, she knew that was what mattered.

Everything else, she would figure out along the way.

ACKNOWLEDGMENTS

First thanks, always, go to Steven Malk, who is the finest agent anyone could ever ask for.

Thanks also to Nancy Conescu for advocating tirelessly on my behalf; to Jessica Shoffel, who might just be the most kickass publicist in the history of publicists; and to everyone at Penguin/Dial for giving my work a home.

Thank you to all the people who gave me up close and personal information about what it's like to live in and love Louisiana and the city of New Orleans, including Lisa Conescu, Stephanie Pellegrin, Owen Pellegrin, Kate Bass, Rachel Bellavia, Jacqueline Goff, Katy Davison Monnot, and Andrea Northrop. Your comments, memories, and observations are woven through every word of this book.

Much gratitude to cherished friends and colleagues

Saundra Mitchell, Stacey Jay, Carrie Ryan, Tonya Hurley, Ellen Hopkins, Tamora Pearce, Lisa Mantchev, Georgia McBride, and Jennifer Draeger.

Heartfelt appreciation to every reader who supports my work, spreads the word, keeps me company online, and encourages me in so many ways, big and small. I like to think you know who you are.

Thanks to my mother, Claudia Baker; my father, Michael St. James; and to Morgan Doyle, Anthony Galazzo, Eileen Cole, and all the people who support and believe in me on a daily basis.

Finally, my deepest gratitude goes to Kenneth, Rebekah, Andrew, and Caroline for all that you do and all that you are. You are my guiding lights.

MICHELLE ZINK (michellezink.com) is a mother of four, living in Pine Bush, New York. She is the author of the Prophecy of the Sisters trilogy and *A Temptation of Angels*.